Jameson's Debt
Forever Midnight MC
Book Four

Victoria Gale

Published in 2020 by

Deryn Publishing

United Kingdom

Second Edition

© 2020 Deryn Publishing

All characters, places and events are fictional. Any resemblance to real persons, places or events is purely coincidental.

The moral rights of the author have been asserted.

All rights reserved. No part of this publication may be reproduced, copied, stored or distributed in any form, without prior written permission of the publisher

VICTORIAGALE

"Not all **families** *are made from blood."*

PROLOGUE

Carina

The second his eyes hit mine, I knew I was in trouble. There was something possessive in his gaze, something dangerous. A rush of fear struck deep in my chest, my vision blurred, and the club whirled around me, a maelstrom of noise and colour. I was used to meeting those some might call bad men. Men who stole and killed and used people to keep themselves in the life they were accustomed to. Hell, my own family had exploited those weaker than themselves for generations. They were no saints, but still, they maintained a certain level of humanity and compassion. They took, but they also gave. The man talking to Gabriel, my brother, had no such traits. I'd never been more certain of anything in my life.

My first instinct was to turn and run, but years of living up to the Rizzo name and upholding the reputation of my family stalled my steps.

I couldn't hear what he was saying, but it was obvious my brother had realised something was wrong when he froze and followed his companion's gaze. A troubled look flashed over his face when he found it resting on me, but he didn't hesitate in stepping in front of the man and blocking his view.

With his gaze no longer burning into me, I took a gasp of air while Gabriel motioned a couple of women, one blonde and the other brunette, to welcome his guest. A pang of guilt formed a lump in my throat at the thought of what those women might be getting themselves into, but I pushed it away. My brother never made any woman do something she wasn't willing to, and they were as free to leave as I was.

With that thought in my mind, and with the strobe lights and the thumping bass now making my head ache, I decided it was best to call it a night.

"Let's get out of here," I said to Rahat as she edged through the crowd toward me and suggested we grab another drink from the bar.

"We've only been here an hour," she said and flicked her lustrous black hair over one shoulder. She looked stunning in her black, strappy catsuit. The sheer mesh bodice left no doubt that Rahat liked to keep in shape, in much the same way the molded bra cups left no doubt that her ample bosom was the result of implants. I looked down at my own natural E cups and wondered why anyone would willingly make their chest the same size as mine. To say they had been the bane of my existence since I turned fourteen would be an understatement. Although, you wouldn't know it with the metallic mini dress I wore that dipped into a deep V at both the front and back, highlighting all my assets.

"Please, let's just go." I reached for her hand. I couldn't leave my friend in the club, not with a man who made my every nerve scream to run away or cower in fear.

Rahat brushed my hand away. "Jeez, Carina. What the hell's gotten into you?"

"It's nothing. I just…" I shrugged and glanced around the club, trying to spot the man with Gabriel again, but at the same time, hoping I wouldn't find him. When I saw him in the VIP section deep in conversation with the blonde, I quickly pulled my eyes away and took Rahat's hand again. "I've got a really bad feeling about tonight. We need to leave. I'll explain at my place. We can watch a movie or something."

She stared at my face, her own burning with questions. After a moment, she huffed out a breath and nodded. "Fine. You win. But can we please grab a bottle or three of Prosecco from the bar to take with us?"

"That, we can do."

Rahat flashed me a beaming smile. "You get the bottles and I'll grab our jackets. We can meet at the front door."

"Thanks, Rahat. But make sure you're there in five," I said, knowing full well that the only reason she'd volunteer to grab the coats was to say goodbye to Tod, who was working tonight in the back office where we'd stashed them.

She winked. "See you in five," she said and disappeared back into the crowd.

I sighed, resisted the urge to glance at the VIP section again, and headed to the bar. A path cleared. Not every customer knew who I was, or that my family owned the place, but the regulars had an idea that I received special treatment at the club. Plus, I normally gave off a vibe showing that I wasn't to be messed with. When a hand snaked around my waist and pulled me backward into a hot and clammy body, I guessed today, with my insides rattled, that vibe was absent.

"Get the fuck off me," I said while trying to break away.

"Come on, love. Just one dance." In his free hand, he held what smelled like a glass of whiskey, only just discernible beneath his stench of BO and booze that stood out amongst the other drinking bodies in the club.

I stifled the roiling in my stomach, stomped on his foot, and elbowed him, forcing him to break his hold and drop his glass.

He cursed and reached to grab me again. A mask of anger flashed over his face. "Fucking stuck-up bitch," he almost spat. "You think you're too good for me."

I was about to come back with an appropriate response when someone beat me to it.

"The lady *is* too good for you," someone said in a voice cold enough to freeze the whiskey puddling on the floor.

Two men grabbed my assailant and dragged him from the club. I almost felt sorry for what would happen to him, but my mind was focused on the man who'd spoken. Gabriel's companion.

Although my legs were weak and my stomach felt like lead, I lifted my gaze to meet his face. To some, he would appear handsome: tall, dark, with full lips, and a strong, defined face that perfectly matched his sun-kissed Italian skin. But, up close, the look he gave me was even more terrifying than it had been from across the room. It was hard to explain what I saw, but it wasn't beauty. It was more a disconcerting mix of hatred, lust, and a need to control.

"Thank you," I said, and moved to turn.

"Thank you, Xander."

"Sorry." I halted my steps.

"My name. Xander Caruso."

I took a deep breath and plastered a smile on my face. "Well, thank you, Xander Caruso. If you'll excuse me." This time, I shut my ears to any potential response, turned and walked to the far side of the bar, as far away from Xander Caruso as I could get. "Nicki," I called the bartender as soon as I arrived. "I'll take three bottles of Prosecco to go." Anxious to be gone quickly, I added, "I'm in a hurry."

Nicki nodded, stopped what she was doing, and grabbed the bottles. She was placing them in a carrier for me when Xander appeared at my side.

"Perhaps I could buy you a drink?" he asked, his commanding voice easily heard above the music.

"I'm actually leaving," I said and resisted a shudder. I hated the way he made me feel weak and powerless when I'd always been confident and self-assured.

"One drink as a way of thanking me properly."

I bristled at this and found some of my usual self, rising to the surface. "I have already thanked you twice. Aside from the fact that I never once asked for your help or needed it, I think that is more than adequate for any service you believe you served. Now, if you'll excuse me."

Nicki gave us both a weary look and placed the bottles on the bar in front of me. I reached up to grab the handle of the carrier, but Xander snatched my hand and held it tight in his own.

"Let go of me," I said, although my mouth was dry and the words hard to come by.

He leaned in close to my ear. "Do I make you nervous?" he asked.

"Nothing makes me nervous," I lied.

He smiled. "Perhaps you are correct and a thank you is not required. However, it is customary and polite to offer someone your name when they give you theirs."

"Fine! My name is Carina Rizzo." The second the words were out of my mouth, I regretted them. The dryness in my throat became unbearable when his smile shifted, and I knew that my name had granted him some extra power over me.

"Rizzo," he said as if to confirm my thoughts. "Of course, I should have seen the family resemblance. Your beauty is very much like your mother's."

"My mother passed away fourteen years ago."

I tried to pull my hand away, but he held it tighter, pulled it to his lips, and brushed a soft kiss that made my skin crawl on the inside of my wrist.

"Which is why it took me a while to register the familial

resemblance," he said, peering at me between his lashes. "Your father passed away soon after if I remember correctly. Not that his death was unexpected. He often crossed the wrong people, and the stress must have taken a toll on his heart. A problem I hope your brother has enough sense to avoid."

My blood boiled. Who the fuck did this man think he was?

"Carina," Nicki called from across the bar. "Do you need me to get the bouncers or your brother?" she asked.

Xander patted my hand and released it. "No need. I'm just leaving. In fact, I'm due to meet with Gabriel shortly." He nodded to the bag holding my bottles of Prosecco. "Have a good evening," he said to me. "I trust we will speak again soon."

"Carina!" What happened to five minutes?" Rahat's voice sounded shrill in my ears as she shouted over the music and emerged from the crowd carrying our jackets. She eyed Xander next to me and a smile played at the edge of her lips. "Oh, I see. If you've changed your mind and would like to stay, that's fine by me."

"No, we couldn't possibly cancel our other engagement," I said, grabbed her arm, and spun her around. I didn't look back as I dragged Rahat to the exit.

As soon as we were out the door and down the steps, she pulled me to a stop. "Carina. What the hell is going on? You are not acting like yourself at all."

I glanced back up at the club entrance. Three doormen covered the door and ushered in the line queuing outside a group at a time. Xander was nowhere to be seen. He hadn't followed me. Not that he needed to with whatever connection he had to my family.

"Carina," Rahat said again. "Speak to me. Is everything alright?"

"That man at the bar--"

"The hot Italian who looked like he wanted to eat you right up?"

I winced at her words. "Yeah, that man."

Rahat handed me my jacket and slipped hers on over her catsuit. "So, what's the problem? You suddenly developed an aversion to drop-dead gorgeous men who clearly have money and want to devour you?"

"Only this one." I thought about her words for a moment and the way Xander sent cold tendrils of fear snaking up my spine. "The problem is," I said, "I can't shake the feeling that this particular man wants to chop me into little pieces with an axe before devouring me, if that makes sense."

"If you're getting a creepy serial killer vibe from him maybe you should talk to Gabriel." She motioned for me to go back inside, but I shook my head.

"Let's just go back to my place for now and open these bottles. Maybe I'm overreacting and all this will seem silly in the morning," I said, knowing full well it wouldn't. Besides, for the first time in my life, I had a feeling Gabriel wouldn't be able to protect me.

We spent the next five minutes flagging down a taxi.

"Frognal, please," I said, climbing in when one finally stopped for us.

We shut the doors, slipped on our seat belts, and pulled away. Rahat pulled one of the bottles from the carrier.

"Do you mind," she asked the driver.

"Not if you're willing to pay for any damages and lost fares for the night if you soil or break anything."

"Deal," Rahat said and popped the cork on the Prosecco.

She took a sip and handed me the bottle. *Why the hell not?* I thought and took an extra-large sip myself. By the time we reached my flat in Hampstead, we'd finished the first bottle and were ready to open a second.

"What have you got to eat?" Rahat asked as we pushed inside, hung our coats on the rack, and took our shoes off so as not to damage the parquet floor.

"Not a lot. Let's finish the second bottle, then order Chinese."

"Sounds like a plan," she said and linked her arm in mine. "Although, let's drink the next bottle out of glasses."

"That might be an idea."

My mind was a million miles away from events in the club when my phone rang.

"I'll pour us a drink," Rahat said and released my arm and toddled toward the kitchen.

"Hello," I said, answering the call.

"Carina, thank fuck you're home. I need you to pack a bag. I've booked you on a flight from Heathrow to New York in four hours. I'll arrange for someone to meet you when you arrive. They'll get you somewhere safe."

I sobered instantly at his words and leaned against the wall, allowing my head to fall back against it. "It's because of Xander Caruso, isn't it?"

Gabriel huffed a breath down the line. "Ah, fuck. I just... I just wish you weren't at the club tonight. Then he would never have seen you."

Not liking the tone that implied somehow this was all my fault, I straightened and said, "I'm at the club every fucking Friday night."

"I know, I know. I'm not blaming you. If I'd had the slightest inclination he was coming, I would have told you to stay home."

Rahat entered the room brandishing two glasses. As soon as she saw my face, she put them on the side table and gave me a questioning look. I pulled the phone away from my mouth and told her what Gabriel had said.

"Serial killer guy?" she asked.

I nodded and returned to the call. "Who the hell is this Xander Caruso?" I asked.

"Let's just say he's a bad man who will stop at nothing to get what he wants. And tonight, he's decided that what he wants is you."

"Well tell him he can't fucking have me."

"Don't you think that's exactly what I've already done?" Gabriel said in a strained voice.

"Then why do I have to run away?"

"Like I said, he's a man who gets what he wants."

"There is no way in hell you are going to New York without me," Rahat said. "I am not leaving your side until this serial killer Xander guy is dealt with."

I pulled the phone away from my mouth. "It's not going to be a fun shopping trip," I said. "I can't ask you to drop everything and hole up in some room for God knows how long."

My friend crossed her arms and gave me her stubborn pose, complete with tapping foot.

"Carina… Carina…" Gabriel's voice came muffled over the line.

"What now?" I said, returning to the phone.

"Did Xander meet Rahat at the club?"

"They didn't exactly meet, but he saw her talking to me, and he knows we left together."

"Then she's going with you whether she wants to or not."

"You can't tell her what to do."

"What did he say?" Rahat asked, picking up her glass and taking a swig.

"He said, you have to come with me whether you want to or not."

"I already said I was bloody coming, Jeez."

I rubbed my head. This three-way conversation was impossible. "If Xander finds me in New York and Rahat is with me, that places her in danger."

"If you disappear and Rahat is left behind for questioning, that places her in even greater danger. As she knows where you're going, her torture and subsequent death at Xander's hands will set him straight on your trail." He said the words in a deadpan voice, and I knew he was serious.

I glanced at my friend. I always worried that her association with me would be her downfall. Now, there could be no doubt.

"What's he saying?" she asked.

I sighed. "We're going to New York," I answered. "Gabriel?"

"Yeah?"

"What about you? Are you going to be alright?"

"I can take care of myself," he answered and fell silent for a few seconds. After a moment, he added. "I'll book Rahat on the same flight as you and email you the details. Get packed and get a taxi to Heathrow as soon as you can. I'll speak to you in a few days when you're safe and settled. Oh, and leave your mobiles. They'll only be good for tracing you now. I'll find another way to contact you."

"Okay. Stay safe," I said.

"You too."

CHAPTER ONE

Jameson

"Me hold the baby," Charlie giggled as soon as Cane entered Caleb's office with Thea, who carried their two-month-old daughter in her arms. She jumped up on the spare chair next to Rex and patted her lap.

Amber came around from behind the desk and held her hand out. "Charlie-baby, how about you, me, Aunt Thea, and Toni-baby go downstairs and leave the men to their boring conversation?" she said. "I'm sure Aunt Thea will let you hold Toni there."

"Okay," Charlie said and jumped up from the seat before grabbing hold of Thea's hand and moving to drag her from the room.

Cane gave Thea a quick peck on the cheek and took the seat Charlie had just vacated. From the corner of my eye, I couldn't help but note the love that shone in Caleb's eyes as they all left.

Lucky passed them as they were on their way out. The last of our group to arrive, he patted Charlie's head in passing and cooed at the baby before perching on the edge of the side unit. I sat on the windowsill and stared outside. The sun stood high in the sky and a warm breeze blasted in my face through the open window.

Lucky cracked a joke about the clubhouse turning into a nursery. Everyone laughed when Cane responded with a quip, implying Lucky was the biggest kid of them all. I smiled. It was weird how close I'd become to each of these men. How much I'd invested in their lives and happiness. I would die for any one of them, and I never doubted they would do the same for me.

Cane and Caleb were blood brothers, but we were all brothers of Forever Midnight MC. Our motorcycle club, our family. I never thought I'd find another after saying goodbye to mine, after turning my back on the family business all those years ago.

Caleb had called the five of us together. The one brother missing, who was usually in attendance at meetings, was Bono, but he was taking a much-needed break to reconnect with his fiancée, Hope.

The laughter died down, and Cane asked, "What's up?" kick-starting the meeting.

"The dispensary up in Fort Collins has been seeing a lot

of trouble of late. Nothing major. Vandalism, broken windows, graffiti. That sort of fucking thing. It started a month or so back, and Bono was going to take a trip and find out what was going on. But we all know that trip got derailed."

"You want me to head up there?" Cane asked.

Caleb shook his head. "I have more sense than trying to drag you away from Thea and the baby. The trip could take anything from a day to more than a couple of weeks. I need you three to go," he said, addressing the last part to me, Lucky, and Rex.

"Not a problem," Rex said. "When do you want us to head out?"

"Yesterday," Caleb said and smiled.

Lucky nodded and stood to leave. Rex followed suit. I shifted on the windowsill.

"What do you expect we'll find?" I asked, curious as to what we weren't being told. We often made trips to check on the brothers' various business interests, but these were normally scheduled in advance. Small things like vandalism would be left to the local chapter to deal with.

Caleb leaned back in his chair and huffed out a breath. "Fuck if I know," he said. "It could be some petty beef, or it could be the first move by a rival group to take over the town. But it seems to be escalating. I'm hoping you'll be able to figure out what the fuck is going on when you get there."

I was about to answer when my phone rang. I pulled it from my jacket pocket. My head instantly throbbed as though it was set to explode when I saw the name 'Jordan' attached to the number. "I gotta take this," I said.

Caleb narrowed his eyes at me but nodded. I wouldn't interrupt the meeting unless it was something serious. I left the room without a backward glance.

Jordan was my blood brother, though none of my new brothers knew that. I wasn't someone who liked to talk about myself or my past. It was something better left buried. My club-brothers had a running joke about the time I turned up at the bar, Midnight Anchor, in a slick suit, looking close to breaking point. The truth was, I was beyond breaking point. The brothers took me in and made me a better person than I ever was before. They gave me a simpler life where things were often black or white and not fifty different shades of gray. They gave me a family I could respect.

I'd avoided anything to do with my birth family for over six years, but need had driven me to contact them, and my brother hadn't hesitated in helping when we needed to protect Hope. Although, that help came with a price tag, a debt owed.

I closed the door behind me, huffed out a deep sigh, and

answered the phone. No doubt, Jordan was calling to collect on that debt.

"What do you want me to do?" I decided to dispense with any formalities.

"It's good to hear your voice, too," Jordan said, unable to keep the bitter tone from his own voice.

"I didn't take this for a social call."

He fell silent for a few seconds, and a vice clamped around my chest. "You remember Xander Caruso?" he asked, and the vice started squeezing ever tighter.

"How could I forget?"

Jordan scoffed, and I knew he was biting back a comment on how I'd forgotten my own family. "Gabriel Rizzo called from London. His sister's in trouble. Caruso wants her big time," he said instead. The vice became too tight, so I sat on the floor and leaned my head against the wall. "She and a friend are due to arrive at J.F.K in eleven hours. Being as you're in the market of protecting women, I need you to keep them safe. Gabriel's sister especially."

I remembered Gabriel's sister from her father's funeral, and her mother's before that. Carina, I think her name was. She was a skinny little kid, drowning in loss and the sea of corruption that surrounded both our families. But she'd stood tall and shook my hand when I'd offered it in condolence for her loss. It rankled me that Caruso had set his sights on her, especially considering his father had been instrumental in her mother's death.

"Send me the details and a recent photo, and I'll be there," I said before adding that I'd text back to confirm if I could make my flight arrangements from Denver and hung up.

I glanced at the door to Caleb's office and shook my head before dragging myself to my feet and going back inside. "My contact in New York is calling in my debt," I said as soon as I entered. All eyes flashed to me. "There are a couple of girls due to arrive in New York. I need to get a flight from Denver within the next few hours."

Caleb stood. "I'll get Amber on it." She worked at the airport and could often book us on a flight at short notice. "Rex is going with you," he added. I was about to object when he raised his hand to still my voice. "This is our fucking debt, not just yours. He's going."

My phone buzzed with a text from Jordan confirming the girls' flight details.

"We need to move fast," I said.

Caleb edged around his desk and moved to leave; we all followed suit. "Lucky," he paused for a moment at the door, "you okay to grab a couple of brothers and head on up to Fort Collins?" he asked, remembering the original reason for our meeting.

"Not a problem," Lucky said, echoing Rex's earlier words.

CHAPTER TWO

Carina

I was exhausted by the time we arrived in New York. Rahat had been all abuzz for the first hour of our flight, and then promptly fell asleep for the rest of the journey. She had woken refreshed with just enough time to head to the toilet and replenish her makeup before the pilot announced our imminent arrival. I hadn't managed a minute's sleep, and not for want of trying. My mind kept drifting back to Xander Caruso and what he would do if he found me. Hell, I didn't even know the man. I wished I'd asked Gabriel more questions. Any questions. I kept imagining that the name Caruso was somehow familiar, but that wouldn't be a surprise. I tried to keep out of the day-to-day logistics of the family business, but I knew most of the key players, and other names were often bandied about. No doubt, Caruso was one of them.

It was a little after 5 a.m. when we collected our bags and

headed outside. My nerves were rising, and I was beginning to worry about who Gabriel would have sent to meet us. There were a few mafia families he worked with in New York. He had contacts everywhere, families allied to our own. I could think of at least two of them to whom my brother might turn for help in the city.

I scanned the thin cluster of people waiting to greet the arrivals and take them to their next destination. A man a few years older than me, at maybe twenty-eight, pushed between me and Rahat, shouting a belated 'Excuse me' after he did so. I mentally forgave him as soon as he ran up to a brunette who was holding a sleepy child and encompassed them both in his arms.

"I don't think anyone's here for us," Rahat said. "Maybe we should get a taxi and check into a hotel in Times Square. We could call your brother from there. Who knows, maybe we could get in a little shopping, after all?"

I sighed, not sure what to do. Rahat's plan was as good as any of our other options. They mostly consisted of standing around and looking confused.

I was about to agree when a firm voice sounded behind me. "Carina Rizzo."

I froze for a second before taking a deep breath and turning. Fuck me!

To say I was surprised to find the sexiest man alive standing before me would be an understatement. He was all muscle and power and screamed sex. My panties flooded just looking at him. He was accompanied by another man, and they were both dressed in jeans and leather biker jackets. I shifted under his gaze. He didn't seem like the type of person my brother would know.

"Carina Rizzo," Mr Sex-on-two-legs said again. I looked him up and down. He was handsome and intense. His deep, midnight eyes burned into me. "Rahat Jones," he added while glancing in her direction before turning his gaze back to me. She eyed him cautiously. Neither of us confirmed our identity. "Our flight leaves in forty minutes," he said. "We should go."

My insides clenched, and I tried to imagine what he looked like without his clothes on. In the movies, men like this were covered in tattoos. I licked my lips and resisted reaching out to run my hand over a chest that seemed made for ink.

His eyes flickered with something for a moment before he turned to leave, while his companion reached out and offered to push the trolley holding our bags.

Unconsciously, I moved to step in line behind him. Rahat grabbed my arm and gave me a pointed look, making me come to my senses.

"We're not going anywhere with you," I said. *What the bloody hell was I thinking?* I didn't know who this guy was from Adam, but if he had the slightest idea that I was going anywhere with someone who looked like they had just stepped out of the TV series *Sons of Anarchy*, he had another thing coming. Even if he had a body that oozed sensuality and power, and intense eyes that made me wet just thinking of them roving over my naked form.

I glanced down and tried to push aside the reactions my body had to his presence, but this only served to highlight them more when I spotted my nipples poking through my T-shirt, demanding to be squeezed.

I suddenly felt very self-conscious that Rahat looked like she'd just stepped from the cover of a magazine while I looked like... well, I looked like a sex-starved nymphomaniac who hadn't slept in more than twenty-four hours and was being plagued by the hangover from hell after imbibing far more Prosecco than was good for me.

I cleared my throat, drew my eyes away from the black T-shirt that did nothing but highlight the firm muscle of his chest, and stared into those magnificent eyes. Doing my best to ignore the trickle of wetness between my legs and my aching core, I stood as tall as humanly possible for someone only five foot, four inches in height, and said, "Who the hell are you and who bloody sent you?" I kept my face blank, but inside I felt a little satisfaction that my voice hadn't wavered.

A slight smile flickered at the edge of his lips. I could almost believe I had imagined it with how quickly it disappeared.

"This is Rex." The other man tipped his head and gave us a warm smile. "You probably don't remember me. My name is Jameson. We last met at your father's funeral."

I studied his face and tried to place it. My brow furrowed. I did recognise this man from the funerals of both my parents. Most of the men in attendance never so much as looked at me, let alone spoke to me, even though I stood next to my brother both times. All their words of comfort had been for Gabriel, but this man had offered me his condolences and shook my hand. He looked different then, younger, most certainly, and his mode of dress had also been remarkably more refined. And as a grieving child, I'd certainly never reacted to him the way my body did now.

"I remember," I said after clearing my throat. "Did my brother ask you to come?"

"He spoke with my brother, Jordan Swash. Jordan asked me to come," he said, and I couldn't help but notice the slight shift in his eyes to his companion when he said this. The Swash family was one of the two I thought my brother would turn to, so instead of asking more questions, I nodded and consented to leave with them.

"You said we were getting on another flight," Rahat said.

"Where are we headed if we're not staying in New York?"

Rex looked at her with a big, beaming smile on his face. "None other than the great Centennial State."

"Where?" Rahat's confusion matched my own.

"Colorado."

"Colorado!" Rahat and I both said at the same time.

Rahat froze in her tracks and folded her arms across her chest. "I'm not being funny," she said, "but are there many people like me in Colorado? You know, of Indian heritage? Like, my grandparents came from *India* heritage."

Rex laughed. "It's not the back of beyond."

"It's not as if you'll be leaving the house when we get there," Jameson added, dampening Rahat's spirits further.

My stomach roiled as I followed Jameson. I was bone tired and hadn't expected to be getting on another flight. I wanted nothing more than a shower and a good ten hours of sleep, but every time I glanced at Jameson, I pictured him in the shower with me.

Rahat and Rex chatted like old friends. Rahat liked to play dumb, but as soon as someone mentioned a computer, she would turn into a complete tech nerd. From the slivers I caught of their conversation, she might have found a soulmate in Rex.

As we boarded the plane to Denver, I tried to stop thinking

about Jameson crawling between my legs and nipping my clit with those perfect teeth, and strove instead to think of what I knew about our destination. I'd been to New York hundreds of times, L.A, and Las Vegas too, but Colorado was a new one for me.

I'd heard it was filled with canyons and high desert plateaus, as well as forested mountains. I remembered, years ago, a friend from university mentioned they were headed there on a skiing trip. But that was the extent of my knowledge.

Jameson's clothes had me thinking too. Not that I minded in the slightest, the way his jeans hugged his tight arse. Fuck, everything about him was so tight and perfect. It's just... his clothes were a long way away from the Armani business suits Gabriel's associates normally wear, and the one Jameson used to wear if memory served. Although, maybe he always dressed like this and put on his Sunday best for the funerals. The leather jacket was a little weird, with a skull sprouting wings and a full moon behind. The words 'Forever Midnight' were written underneath. Rex had the same emblem on his jacket.

I shook my head, trying to dislodge the notion that they might be involved in a weird cult or something. That shifted my thoughts to hoping it was a sex cult where Jameson would tie me up and tease me 24-7. *What the hell is wrong with me?* More likely, the clothing was part of a planned disguise to keep us safe. I looked down at my Dior jeans and T-shirt and decided that Rahat and I might be overdressed.

I racked my brain, trying to remember all I knew about the Swash family. I'd seen Jordan a time or twenty when he'd visited my brother over the last ten years, but Jameson never accompanied him, which made him something of a mystery, especially as I believed Jameson was the older of the two brothers. He had the same strong and angular jawline as his brother, and they were both tall, but physically, that was where the similarity between them ended. Jameson was the larger of the two, bulked with muscles instead of the sleek lines his brother possessed. Although his waist looked just about perfect for wrapping my legs around.

I let my gaze travel his body and decided I needed to know everything there was to know about him, and to see every inch.

"Rahat," I said as soon as we boarded the plane to Denver, "will you be okay next to Rex for a while? I need to talk to Jameson."

Rahat glanced at Rex, who once again beamed at her. She laughed and confirmed she'd be just fine.

I took a deep breath and glanced around the cabin. Only half of the seats were occupied on the flight, and our group was not seated close to any other passengers.

"I'll take the aisle," Jameson ushered me to take the window seat. "You have questions," he said as soon as we were comfortable or, at least, gave the outward appearance of being that way.

My mouth suddenly became very dry, and I licked my lips. Jameson shifted his gaze as though refusing to look at me and stared at the monitor on the back of the chair in front of him. I swallowed quickly, feeling like I'd been caught doing something wrong.

Jameson no doubt thought me a fool, all but demanding to sit with him, and then being lost for words. I huffed out a breath and shook my head again.

What the fuck was I doing, and why the hell should I care what he thinks of me? No matter that his slightest glance sent bolts of need straight to my core. Maybe it was for the best that he stared straight ahead. I'd be wise to do the same.

"I want to know what you know about Xander Caruso," I said, more of a statement than a question. "And why my brother needed to send me away?" They might not be my intended words, but the questions were ones I needed answers to.

Jameson didn't respond at first, and I wasn't sure if I should rephrase my statements as questions or if he was simply mulling over his response. After a moment, he said, "Have you ever met Xander Caruso?"

"Yes."

"Then you have your answer."

I stared at him, dumbfounded for a minute. *What the hell was that supposed to mean?* "No, I don't," I said, a note of incredulity in my voice.

Jameson leaned his head back against the chair and gusted a deep breath out of his nostrils. "When you met Caruso, did you get the impression he was a nice man?"

"You sure like to answer a question with another question, don't you?" I asked. Jameson looked at me, and I saw that quick flash of a smile at the corner of his lips again. He brushed his hand under his chin, and I imagined it brushing under mine, lifting my head higher for him to kiss me. I turned my gaze away again, and said, "No. He was most definitely not a nice man. But I could have handled him," I added, even though I knew that wasn't true.

"Do you think I'm a nice man?"

The unexpected question caught me off guard.

My stomach flip-flopped. What I thought was that he was a man I wanted to do dirty things with. "My brother wouldn't have trusted you to keep me safe, if you weren't," I said, pushing away thoughts of him spanking my bottom.

He reached across the chair and dragged the tip of his finger across my lips, dragging my bottom one down. My heart pounded and my insides clenched as thoughts of his cock pounding in and out of my mouth flooded my mind.

"You've the body of a woman now, but you're still a naïve little girl at heart."

He pulled away, and my heart sank to the pit of my stomach. I bristled at his comments, grabbed the headphones provided by the airline, and slapped them on my head to block out any further attempt at conversation with music. Turning to look out the window, I ignored the new flood of wetness in my panties, and resolved I'd damn well show him just how much of a woman I'd become.

CHAPTER THREE

Jameson

As I'd intended, Carina turned away from me in a huff.

It had been a shock to see the little girl I met all grown up in the photograph Jordan sent me, and an even bigger shock to see her in person. Any thoughts of her still being a little girl fled in an instant. She was full of delicious, natural curves. And the way she looked at me… fuck… those eyes flashed with a myriad of emotions all at once. And those lips, all pouty and kissable. She had me imagining just what it would feel like to explore those curves with my tongue.

The rest of the flight seemed to take an age. I couldn't get the image of Carina tied spread-eagled to my bed with my tongue, exploring every inch of her pussy, out of my head. The journey from the airport to the safe house seemed to take even longer. She was still pretending to be pissed at me. But the look in her eyes said otherwise and made my cock twitch to life in my pants. I shifted in my seat, and Rex gave me a knowing smirk from the passenger seat. Fucking juvenile. Like he hadn't had a stiffy the entire time he'd been talking to Rahat.

I growled under my breath and shook my head. I may have wanted nothing more than to thrust my engorged cock in and out of her tight pussy, but I was here to keep her safe. Nothing more. Nothing less. Besides, I'd said goodbye to my family because of the backstabbing and drama, because of too many games being played. Carina Rizzo was nothing but a big fucking time bomb full of exploding drama. I just wished my fucking cock would realize it.

A little after midday, we pulled up outside the safe house as it was fast becoming known. A colonial-style farmhouse set among a few acres of land. It was one of a number of properties in the portfolio my brother and I inherited, and had been my original destination when I'd decided to settle in Colorado for a while. That had been more than seven years ago. I'd never made it to the house then. Meeting the brothers of Forever Midnight saw me settling in Castle Rock instead. We'd originally used the house to keep Amber hidden away from the leader of a rival motorcycle club; an act that reconnected me with my brother. I'd needed his help again to save Hope, Bono's fiancée. He'd believed her long dead, but in reality, she'd been placed in Witness Protection after witnessing a Mafia hit. Those steps led me to the debt I was repaying today, and I couldn't help but feel that my new life was connecting in far too many ways with my old one.

Carina and Rahat jumped out of the car as soon as it came to a halt. Rex and I grabbed their bags and directed them inside. Carina glanced back at me, biting her bottom lip and smiling.

"Nice place," she said, having obviously given up on the idea of pretending to be pissed.

I growled and tried not to look at the sway of her hips as they wagged back and forth.

The ladies freshened up. After that, Rex gave them a tour of the property while I searched the cupboards and fridge to see if we had any food. We'd only decided to come to the safe house on the flight to New York and hadn't arranged for any supplies to be provided. I debated calling Caleb and asking if he could have one of the brothers make a run to the store for us, but Rex volunteered as soon as he came back inside.

"Oh, me too," Rahat collapsed onto his arm.

Rex couldn't keep the grin from his face, and I knew neither of them planned on spending the night alone.

"Not a chance. You'll be too conspicuous," I said, ignoring the look Rex gave me.

"Let her go," Carina said. "There's no way Xander could know we're even in the States yet. This may be her last chance to get out of the house."

From the look both Rex and Rahat gave me, I knew they wanted some time alone. I also knew Carina was right. I grumbled and shook my head, worried that my reluctance in letting Rahat leave was more about my concern at being left alone with Carina. "Fine," I said after a moment. "But make it a quick trip. Don't call home and don't draw any attention to yourselves."

Rahat almost shrieked in delight before turning to Carina. "Do you want to come?" she asked, but Carina shook her head and said she was staying right here with me. Damn right she was. Although, the look she gave me couldn't have been any clearer, making my concerns grow.

As soon as the others left, she asked me for a glass of water. I reached into the cupboard and removed a glass before pouring her a drink from the tap.

I handed her the water, but instead of taking it, she clasped her hand around mine and stepped in close, eyeballing me suggestively.

Nothing but a fucking time bomb! I reminded myself. I should have pulled away and left the room. But I wasn't about to walk away and keep things hanging in the air between us. So help me, I had to nip whatever this was in the bud. There could never be anything between us. She was too much a part of my old life, and I wanted nothing more to do with it.

I lifted her chin, so our eyes met. "I don't play games," I said.

"Neither do I," she answered before she placed the glass on the counter and planted her lips on mine, never breaking our gaze.

CHAPTER FOUR

Carina

Jameson kissed me back, sending molten fire flooding deep to my core. I knew he would. His attraction to me was as clear as my own to him. We kissed deep and fast. His tongue explored my mouth. My heart raced. A desperate need to feel his cock overwhelmed me.

I slipped my hands into his jeans, opened them, and delved inside. I gasped when I felt the size of him against my fingers. He grew even thicker and engorged as I touched him.

"You don't know what you're starting," he whispered and pushed me away a little.

I licked my lips. "I know what I want."

I squeezed tighter, and he growled. Before I knew it, his hand snaked around my head and into my hair. His fist closed tight at my scalp, and he wrenched my head back sharply. I gasped and let go of his cock. My panties became wetter.

His lip curled, and this time, there was no missing the smile at its edge or the glint in his eyes. He looked ready to strip me bare, and I wanted… I needed him to. I wanted to stand in front of him naked and exposed, with his eyes roving over every inch of my body. His hands, his tongue, exploring every inch of me. And I knew he wanted it, too. That's why when he growled and pulled away from me, my immediate reaction was one of surprise, which quickly turned to anger.

"What the hell?" I said, my voice more shrill than I would have liked.

"I'm here to keep you safe," Jameson said and moved around the counter towards the back door. "Not to keep you entertained. I'm not your plaything, and as I said, I don't play games."

"You could have fooled me." He'd kissed me back. He wanted me as much as I wanted him. He'd pushed me away on the aeroplane, and he was doing the same now. And still, he had the audacity to say he doesn't play games, as if I'm the one playing them. I wanted to scream, or better yet, punch him in the face. My fists tightened, but before I could do anything, he opened the back door and stormed into the garden, slamming it behind him.

I watched him through the window; his face was tense when

he pulled his phone from his pocket. He turned his back to the house, and I inched forward, opening the door to hear his call.

"What the fuck have you got me into?" he asked into the phone. I bristled. I could ask the same fucking thing.

Anything else he said was lost as he moved towards the electric fence that surrounded the property, apparently a new addition to their security measures. There were cameras everywhere and Rex had delighted in showing us around. Our tour had included a large safe room boasting a bulletproof door and an armoured multi-point locking system. The place looked cosy, with a large brown leather sofa, a TV, a laptop, and bookcases. That was until Rex opened one of the cupboards to show us the small portable toilet and another to demonstrate how we would need to turn our oxygen on and off. I couldn't even fathom a situation where such a room would be needed, and the thought of being locked in the windowless prison sent chills up my spine and filled me with dread.

I closed the back door softly and turned to look around the kitchen. My stomach rumbled, and I wished I'd gone with Rahat. Anything would be better than being stuck in this house.

I was about to go upstairs and scream into a pillow when the front door crashed open, making a weight like a lead ball sink into my stomach. I froze, not knowing where to go or what to do. The safe room was an option, but Jameson was closer. Neither sounded appealing at that moment in time.

"Carina."

A rush of relief at the sound of Rahat's voice had me gusting out a breath of air. A second later, the kitchen door banged open and Rex dragged Rahat in by her arm. The look on both their faces told me something was wrong.

"Where's Jameson?" Rex demanded. I nodded towards the back door, and Rex pushed Rahat towards a breakfast stool. "Sit there and wait," he said and left.

"What happened?" I asked.

"Rex is a fucking arsehole is what happened," Rahat answered. "We didn't get a mile down the road when he got all uppity about my mobile--"

"Your mobile!" My heart sank. "I told you to leave it at home. You know what's at risk."

"I don't know anything and neither do you," she said, but had the decency to look ashamed while she said it.

When Jameson barged through the back door with Rex in tow a moment later, I stepped in front of my friend. He scowled, but he stilled his charge and the look on his face softened, just about. I hoped that meant Rahat was out of any danger.

He edged around the kitchen island and stood opposite her, his nostrils flaring. After a second, he uncrossed his arms and slammed Rahat's mobile and its battery on the counter. "When and where have you used it?" he asked.

Rahat looked at me and then stared at her phone without answering.

Rex cleared his throat. "She had the battery out, but put it in and powered up in the car before I had the chance to stop her."

"Enough time for someone to get a trace?"

Rex shrugged and turned to Rahat. "That depends."

Rahat scowled at him. "I'm not stupid," she said. "I disabled all the apps that use location services before leaving London. Plus, I turned it on aeroplane mode and removed the battery."

"Did you disable the GPS?" Rex said.

"Yes, I disabled the GPS."

Jameson leaned back against the counter and ran his hand over the top of his head; his lips clamped together in a hard line. "Then we should be clear?" he said to Rex, who nodded. Jameson shifted and moved closer to the counter within arm's reach of Rahat.

She shifted under his gaze, but stared at him defiantly. "You're all fucking crazy," she said. "This Xander guy doesn't even know who I am. He saw me with Carina for like five seconds, and you know what, he seemed a damn sight nicer than you do."

Jameson leaned on his elbows on the counter and moved his face closer to Rahat. Without moving his eyes from hers, he said, "Did he now? I know Xander Caruso. I had to clean up after one of his messes. We were in London and some guy bumped into him in a pub and called him a prick. Do you know what he did?"

Rahat gulped and shook her head.

"He broke his kneecaps. Cut his fingers off one by one. After that, he burned his eyes out with battery acid. You want to know how I found him?"

"That's enough," I said.

"With his dick shoved down his throat. Xander had cut it off and used it to choke him to death." I swallowed back the lump forming in my throat and tried to ignore the nausea churning my stomach. Jameson tilted his head to the side and continued. "Xander was never a *nice* man, but that was the day I learned the sort of man he truly was. Funnily enough, it was also the day I learned that prick was British slang for penis, but you already know that. Do you want to know what else he's capable of?"

"No. That's enough," I said again. "She gets it."

"Do you?" Jameson asked.

Rahat nodded, and tears formed in her eyes. Her mouth

dropped open as if to say something.

"She gets it," I said, my anger growing along with my fear. "You didn't have to say any of this crap."

Jameson turned his attention to me. "You *both* need to know that this isn't a game. Rex and I are here to protect you. Xander Caruso may be after you, Carina, but he won't hesitate to go through Rahat to find you. I just spoke to my brother. Xander left London for New York about an hour ago. There's no way in hell Gabriel or Jordan told him where to head, but he found out someho--"

"I connected to the Wi-Fi just before we arrived in New York," Rahat said, her voice wavering. She turned to look at Rex. "In the aeroplane toilet. I just wanted to check messenger."

"They could have tracked it through the MAC address," Rex said and shook his head. "To connect to the Wi-Fi, you would have had to turn aeroplane mode off and enabled Wi-Fi. Did you disable Wi-Fi and switch aeroplane mode back on afterwards?"

Rahat stared at her phone on the counter before her. "I-I'm not sure," she said after a moment. "There was an announcement to say we were landing and that we should get back to our seats. I popped the battery, but I just don't know. I-I might not have. There's no way to be sure without turning the phone back on," she added.

Jameson growled and rubbed his hand over his head again. "Get your things. We're leaving," he said.

"What? We've been on the go for days." I couldn't stomach having to leave and go somewhere else, especially cooped up in the car with Jameson, and I had no doubt Rahat felt the same way about Jameson and Rex.

"We're leaving," Jameson said again and scooped Rahat's phone and battery up from the counter. "Rex, make sure everything's locked up."

With that, he left the kitchen. His footsteps sounded on the stairs, and I wondered where the hell we were going to go now.

Rahat grabbed my hand. "I'm sorry, Carina. The odds of someone tracking my phone, it just… it didn't seem believable. And the MAC address with the Wi-Fi… Who the fuck are these people?"

I patted her hand and gave her a weak smile while guilt gnawed away at my insides. Rahat may have been foolish with her phone, but I'd dragged her into a situation she could never have hoped to comprehend. She didn't live my life, and the truth was, I barely took note of it myself. These people were my family. They were mafia. They would keep us safe because of the ties my family had to the Swash family, but I could only imagine how far those ties would hold.

"I'm not coming with you," Rahat said as she reached out and grabbed my hands.

"It's not safe--"

"I know. I understand that now. Which is why I've got to fix the mess I created." I opened my mouth to protest, but she raised her hand and silenced me. "Trust me. I have an idea."

CHAPTER FIVE

Carina

"I need to know what's going on," I said to Jameson as he steered away from the house.

Rahat and Rex had left in one of the spare vehicles found in the ample garage with a plan to head to Los Angeles. Rahat had come up with the idea that she could act as a decoy. To say I wasn't happy with the idea was an understatement, but Rex assured me he would keep her safe. In LA, they would reactivate the phone, and Rahat would post a few pictures on social media showing where she was. After that, they would leave the phone in California and head back to join us. Hopefully, Xander would think I was with Rahat and head there, but just in case, Jameson and I were leaving the safe house until we had a better idea of Xander's location.

Jameson glanced at me, but kept silent.

I sighed and shook my head before flopping it back on the headrest. "I am just so tired of all of this crap," I said.

Jameson growled a laugh under his breath. "I can relate to that."

"Then tell me what's going on. Please. It's just ridiculous to think that Xander Caruso saw me for like five seconds and suddenly decided I was his." I glanced out the window and looked at the mountains in the distance. It was hard to imagine Xander finding me here. It was hard to imagine being here. I'd travelled extensively, but always to cities, bristling with people and buzzing with atmosphere. I'd always thought the lights were beautiful, but they were nothing compared to the vast natural world surrounding me. I just hoped I'd live to see more of this world. "I get that he's a nutjob," I said, continuing, "but it doesn't make any sense." Sure, I wasn't bad to look at, but it wasn't as if I had magical powers that made all the boys fall madly in love with me.

Jameson took a deep breath. I could see the fight going on behind his eyes.

"Please," I said again. "I need to know."

"It's not my place to tell you."

"Then let me call my brother. I can't go on like this."

"You can call him as soon as we get where we're going. We'll be able to establish a safe line."

I wanted to growl in frustration, to punch the dashboard. Jameson was as bad as my brother. He knew more than he was saying, but just like everyone else my entire life, he wanted to keep me in the dark. When I met him all those years ago at his father's funeral, I thought he was different from all the other men my family worked with. He'd seen me. I so desperately needed him to see me now.

I thought back to my brief meeting with Xander. He'd mentioned how much I looked like my mother. It was true, everyone said so, and I saw the familiarity of myself from photos.

"Does this have anything to do with my mum?" I shook my head. "Ignore me. She had to be twenty years older than him." He was surely too young to remember her well.

Jameson grumbled and thrummed his hand on the steering wheel a couple of times, before indicating and turning onto a side street. "His dad had a creepy obsession with your mother. Manuel, Xander's father, was in competition with your dad for her hand. At the time, the power dynamic between your families was equal. The consigliere who mediated the dispute decided your mother had the right to choose who she wanted to marry. She chose Petra Rizzo, your father. Manuel married someone else, but the Carusos are known to hold a grudge."

"But that wasn't the end of it," I said as a rock sank into the pit of my stomach.

"No. When Manuel became second in command, the power dynamic between your families shifted. Manuel left his wife and demanded that your mother leave your father." Jameson huffed out a deep breath and flashed his gaze to mine before returning it to the road. "She refused and Manuel made both their lives miserable because of it. From the little I know, that's when your mother started drinking. She loved your father and the family they had together. She wanted to stay, but a part of her knew it would be better for all of you if she left."

Tears flooded my eyes at his words. I'd been so young. I knew Mum had been drinking a lot, but she was always happy and smiling around me. I could never have imagined what was going on underneath. After her accident, Dad had fallen into a depression and died when his heart gave out. "Why didn't anyone tell me this before?" I asked, wiping away my tears.

Jameson shrugged. "You were young. Your mother's death was an accident, and your father died of a broken heart. Maybe Gabriel just decided there was no reason for you to know more than that."

I sniffed back tears at his words as my anger flared. "They were my parents. My family. I had a right to know. Everything I remember from my childhood was a lie."

"Your mother and father loved each other. They loved you and

Gabriel. There was no lie in that."

I glanced out the window. The sun blossomed red and gold as it moved behind the mountains. Darkness would arrive soon. I'd lost track of how long I'd been awake, but sleep seemed like an impossible dream. "So what? I'm supposed to be a plaything for the son of the man who destroyed my family."

"No. Not a plaything. Jordan said that Xander has claimed you as his wife. A union between your families that was denied to his father."

"His wife! This is fucking bullshit! I'm not going to marry that psycho." I ran my hand over my head and resisted punching the window. My mind raced as I tried to muddle through all I'd learnt. "What about this mediator?" I asked. "This consigliere guy? Can't I appeal to him? If my mother had the right to choose, shouldn't I be granted that same right?"

"The role of consigliere has been vacant for a long time." Jameson cleared his throat and kept his eyes firmly on the road. "The power dynamic is also different now. Manuel is the underboss of our connected families. He's second in command to the big boss himself and takes commands from no-one except Don Bianchi himself."

I sniffed loudly. Jameson placed his hand on my leg. I almost jumped at the unexpected touch. I felt lost and scared and had the weight of the world on my shoulders, but under the warmth of his hand I wanted nothing more than for him to gather me in his arms and promise to keep me safe… to fuck me blind. But I knew such a thing wasn't possible. No wonder he pulled back in the kitchen, even though I knew he wanted me as much as I wanted him. I was already taken.

"What happens now?" I asked.

"I keep you safe until Gabriel and Jordan figure things out."

"And if they don't?"

He didn't respond to that. Instead, he pulled his hand from my leg and turned onto a road signposted as leading to Castle Rock.

CHAPTER SIX

Jameson

C arina's nerves were on edge when I buzzed open the security gates and drove into the parking lot of the clubhouse.

A few of the brothers waved their hands at me or nodded their heads in greeting. A few eyed Carina with lust-filled eyes, making my blood boil. My hands clenched on the steering wheel. I resisted a growl, hating that I felt possessive of her.

Carina must have noticed my tension and misread my mood. Her nerves grew, though she tried not to show it. Her breaths came quick, and her eyes darted around the lot, taking in the Harleys, Triumphs, Choppers, and BMWs. The air was filled with the rev of engines and the smell of petrol.

"Where are we?" she asked, shifting in her seat.

"The Forever Midnight clubhouse," I answered.

"Like the name on your jacket."

"Exactly."

She let out a growl of frustration, as if she wanted a better answer than that, but she would be moving on soon enough and didn't need to get too close to the brothers or know their business.

Carina scanned the clubhouse as we entered. There were people everywhere. A few called my name or fist-bumped me as I walked past. I glanced around, thankful that the club had changed a lot in the last year or so. With both Cane and Caleb settling down with kids, dolly girls who frequented the club weren't as out in the open as they used to be. Don't get me wrong, most brothers still liked fucking anyone with a pair of tits, but it happened in the bunkhouses, behind closed doors, and not in the main room now.

A part of me wished I'd been able to take her straight to my place and avoid the glances and glares of the brothers, but we needed the safety of the clubhouse and the protection it offered. At least, that's what I told myself. It had nothing to do with the fact that I didn't entirely trust myself to be alone with Carina. She'd been so vulnerable in the car, so scared of what the future might hold. I'd just wanted to lift her in my arms, take her home, and fuck her until she forgot all her worries. I'm not sure who was more surprised when I'd put my hand on her leg, me or her. Her eyes had burned with questions and need... *Fuck!* The sooner she was out of my life, the better.

"This way," I said and led Carina through the clubhouse and up to Caleb's office.

He stood as soon as we entered, reached his hand out to Carina, and guided her to one of the chairs surrounding his desk.

"I'm glad you're safe," he said and offered her some food. She accepted, so Caleb called one of the brothers and told him to fetch a burger and a drink.

"What the fuck happened?" he asked me as soon as I sat down in the chair next to Carina's.

He shook his head as I explained the mix-up with the phone and that Rex had headed to LA with Rahat. "I'll call Bono and Lucky home. Bono especially will be fucking pissed if we don't. We owe your contact a world of debt after he helped us save Hope."

"I'd like to talk to Gabriel," Carina said just as the brother returned with a burger and fries, as well as a glass of water, and three shots of whisky. He handed the plate to Carina, who thanked him, and put the glasses on Caleb's desk before leaving. "If that's not possible," Carina continued, "then maybe we could speak to your brother. Jordan might have an idea of what's going on and where Xander is."

I stiffened at her words and glanced at Caleb. He hadn't known that Jordan was my blood-brother. I should have come clean and shared my past with him when I had the chance. He'd never pushed for an answer, never asked who or what I was running from. While Carina popped a fry in her mouth, and moaned as if it was the best fucking thing she'd ever tasted, Caleb gave me an almost imperceptible nod of his head, and his lips turned up in a slight smile. We were good. At least for now, but I owed it to all my brothers to tell them the truth of who I was.

Before I had the chance to say anything, Cane arrived with Amber.

"Where's Charlie?" Caleb asked as Amber walked around the desk and pulled him in for a deep kiss.

Cane nodded in greeting to Carina, who placed her plate of food on the desk and swallowed the morsel in her mouth self-consciously. He flashed her a cheeky grin, something I'd never have thought him capable of before he'd met Thea. He grabbed one of her fries before popping it in his mouth. "She's at my place with Thea and Toni," he said and stole another fry. "I'm fucking starving."

Caleb pulled Amber down onto his lap and snaked his arms around her waist. "Does that mean we have the night all to ourselves?" he asked with a devilish grin on his face.

Amber sealed his lips with another kiss before pulling back. "It does," she said, "or at least, we will." She gave Carina a warm smile and introduced herself.

"I'm sorry to intrude," Carina replied as Cane grabbed another fry from her plate.

"Go get your own," Amber said and leaned forward, slapping Cane's hand playfully away from the plate. "You look exhausted," she said to Carina as he left the room.

"It's been a long day or two or three." Carina rubbed the back of her neck and smiled. "I feel like I could sleep for a week."

"I can imagine." Amber shook her head. "Getting off a flight from London and straight on another to Colorado couldn't have been easy."

"Amber arranged the plane tickets," I said by way of explanation for her knowledge of the journey.

"I did. I also know from experience that these guys can go days without sleep and have no concept of how tiring things can be." She stood and held one hand out to Carina while picking up the plate of food with the other. "Come on, I'll get you settled. Somewhere warm and comfy while these guys talk."

Carina stiffened a little, but shook off her tension as soon as she took Amber's hand. They left the room together, arm in arm like old friends, while Caleb picked up the phone.

"I'll call Bono and Lucky," he said just as Cane entered with his own burger and fries. "Lucky can be back in a few hours and Bono the day after tomorrow."

"Leave them. Bono needs his time with Hope, and Lucky needs to find out what's going on in Fort Collins. Carina will be safe here for now." I sat forward in my chair and placed my head in my hands before shaking my head and grunting. "About Jordan."

"Your brother." Caleb said.

"My brother," I agreed. "He's the head of the Swash family. They're... we're a mafia family based out of New York. Until the trouble with Amber, I hadn't spoken to him in almost seven years."

Cane swallowed a bite of his burger and lifted his chin. "We always knew you had a past. It makes no difference to us what that past is. Not all families are made from blood," he said. "Whatever beef is between you and your older brother, you'll have our support."

I huffed out a deep breath. "Jordan's my younger brother. He took over as head of the family when I stepped down."

CHAPTER SEVEN

Jameson

It was hard to keep my eyes off Carina when we left the clubhouse and drove to Bono's place the next morning. I itched to reach out and brush her long, dark hair from her bare shoulder. I wanted to feel the touch of her soft olive skin beneath my fingers... my lips.

We'd spent the early hours having breakfast with Cane, Caleb, and Amber. Thea and the kids also joined us after a while. Until we were able to return to the safe house, Amber would host Thea and the kids at her and Caleb's house, and Caleb would lodge at Cane's place with him and a couple of brothers. Bono's cabin was off the beaten track, surrounded by forests and mountains, but anyone who tried to reach it would have to pass Cane's first. We'd be safe there for a while.

I focused on the road and tried to keep my thoughts away

from how perfect Carina was and how much my body reacted to her presence.

It had been strange watching her interact with my brothers. I'd always worried about my two worlds colliding. I still did, but Carina had laughed at all their jokes, and generally seemed at ease in their company. She was used to being around powerful and dangerous men, but the men she dealt with dressed their power in designer suits, slick haircuts, and manicures. With the brothers, what you saw was what you got. They were rough around the edges and not afraid to punch someone in the face if they stepped out of line. But they only hurt people who deserved it, and once they claimed you as family, they would fight to the death to keep you safe.

"I can understand why you like it here so much," she said, her gaze focused out the window. "Everything is so beautiful, and you have friends... I mean, like real friends."

I knew what she meant. I thought I had friends in my previous life, but I only had people jostling for position and seeing what they could get out of their association with me. They were people who would talk nice to my face, but stab me in the back as soon as the opportunity arose. "Like Rahat?" I asked while trying not to stare at the way her lilac bra strap was visible beneath her strappy vest, which hugged all her curves and highlighted her cleavage.

"Exactly like Rahat." Carina's gaze flashed to her lap, and she took a deep, pained breath. "Rahat didn't know about any of this," she added, her voice quiet. "She thought I was some spoiled rich kid whose brother owns a nightclub. We've been friends for half our lives, but I never told her the truth. I never told her what my family was capable of. When... when you mentioned what Caruso did in London, how he killed that guy. It sounds so silly, but I was more worried that Rahat would look down on my family because of our association with men like him more than I was of him finding me."

I scoffed. I could relate to that. "She seems to care for you. She wouldn't have been willing to put herself at risk if she didn't."

Carina turned to face out the window again, but not before I saw a tear glint in her eye. "I'm the one who put her at risk. I should have told her the truth a long time ago. I should have pushed her away and kept her safe from my world."

I opened my mouth to say something when the deafening screech of tires sounded behind us, drawing my attention. At first, I wondered if it might be some brothers, but a quick glance showed me it was the Feral Sons. They'd kept to themselves since their leader, Leo, went after Amber for the second time in order to hurt Caleb. Leo had been killed by the local police. The rest of the gang had stayed well clear of Castle Rock and the brothers since then, but from the way they rushed forward to tailgate the

Jeep and bunched around us, it was clear that the situation had changed.

Carina yelped when one of the bikes pulled alongside, and its driver tapped on her window. I growled and put my foot down, knowing there was no way we could get away from all the bikes, and cursed the vulnerable situation I'd placed us in. They had us boxed in. The rearview window and every side window were full of the vision of spinning wheels, flashing leather, and jeering faces.

"Friends of yours?" Carina asked, shouting to be heard above the roar and rev of engines.

"Not exactly." I glanced at the road ahead. We were still in town. A couple of people rushed along the sidewalk up ahead and ducked inside a barber shop. I huffed an angry breath out of my nostrils and clenched my jaw. My brothers in Forever Midnight would hear of the presence of the Feral Sons within minutes. It would take at least another five for them to gather and get on their bikes and reach us. If we were lucky.

A sudden pop, pop, pop sounded close enough to burst my eardrums. Carina screamed and ducked down in her seat, but the shower of bullets had been aimed at my head. Thank fuck, the Jeep was armored. I didn't know what the Feral Sons were playing at, but something told me Xander Caruso had a hand in their actions.

If that was true, then he knew where Carina was and no amount of staged photographs in Los Angeles would shake him from her trail.

I gripped the steering wheel and floored the gas with little hope of outrunning them. The top speed of the bikes easily matched that of the Jeep, and in the built-up area of the town, their maneuverability was greater than mine. My options were limited. But I did have bulk on my side. I lurched the Jeep to the side, swiping three of the bikes and taking them out of the game in the process. I tried to do the same on the left, but they were ready for me.

Without warning, the bikes disengaged from their lockstep of the Jeep. I corrected my course and stayed on the road, but the distraction had served to take my focus away from the side street. It was too late to react when I noticed the SUV charging toward us. It turned at the last second and clipped the front of our vehicle. I lost control, and the Jeep went into a tailspin, only to be clipped again. This time, the Jeep flipped.

I clenched my jaw, braced one hand on the roof, and reached out to pin Carina in her seat with the other. We were both wearing seatbelts, but even so, it felt as if we bounced around the car like pinballs in a pinball machine. Carina's eyes locked with mine, and my heart ached at the fear inside them.

It seemed like the Jeep bounced for an eternity before finally coming to an abrupt stop against the side of a laundromat. It was by sheer dumb luck that we'd landed upright with the wheels beneath us. Smoke billowed out of the engine, and from the burning smell that accompanied it, I knew we had no hope of driving away as if nothing had happened.

Whoops and hollers sounded outside. One of the Feral Sons stepped from his bike and walked towards us, pointing the gun at my head.

"We just want the girl," he said, reinforcing my suspicion that Caruso had to be involved. I glanced at Carina, who'd gone as white as a sheet. She had a slight scratch on her cheek, and her hair was disheveled, but all in all, we'd both come out of the accident relatively unscathed.

Carina's breath seemed to catch in her throat. "What do we do?" she asked, her voice no more than a whisper.

I flipped open the glove compartment and searched inside for my phone. We were still inside the bubble of the Jeep, but I didn't think it would take many shots to break through the glass. Plus, the hiss, smoke, and smell of gas and oil coming from the engine had me worried we could catch fire or explode at any minute. My hand landed on my phone. I cursed. The screen was smashed, and the touchscreen was inoperable. I tossed it to the floor just as a commotion broke out on the street.

The few Feral Sons who'd dismounted were all running back to their bikes. Gunshots fired. They pulled away from the Jeep, rushing down the street to escape the Forever Midnight brothers that chased after them. A thunderous roar rumbled past us as the brothers drove them away.

Lucky appeared, grinning with a cheeky smile on his face. "Saved by the cavalry," he said before asking if we were both okay to walk.

I jumped from the Jeep and motioned for Carina to do the same. "Took your fucking time," I said, returning his smile.

"You know me. I always like to keep things fucking interesting." He motioned with his head at the brothers chasing the Feral Sons out of town before reaching into his jacket and retrieving a gun. "We'll take care of these guys. You head to Ma's. I'll see you there when I can."

The second I took the gun from his outstretched hand, Lucky spun his bike around and continued his pursuit.

"We go this way," I said and pointed along the far end of the road while reaching for Carina's hand. We rushed past a liquor store, an auto shop, and a farm store. I pulled Carina close, practically dragging her along behind me while making sure we stayed close to walls and the edge of the buildings. I couldn't see anyone following, but that didn't mean no one was there. Two blocks over, we ducked into an alleyway, which emerged in a residential area. "Not far now," I said, but Carina only nodded in return. Her breathing was labored and her hand shook within mine. I worried she might be going into shock, but it was more likely she was coming out of an adrenaline rush. Neither scenario was a good one.

We rounded the corner and darted through a playground. I felt a pang of relief at the sight of Kitty's place, two houses down. I scanned the neighborhood, watching one last time for prying eyes before dashing across the road, running up to Kitty's door and banging.

"What the fuck is going on?" Kitty asked as soon as she opened the door to her ranch style home, but her question was forgotten as soon as she saw Carina. She rushed forward and scooped her arm around her shoulders. "Let's get you inside, honey," she said and scowled at me. "For fuck's sake, get the girl a glass of water."

CHAPTER EIGHT

Carina

I thought I might pass out by the time we reached the house. My heart pounded, and my mind swam. I couldn't grasp onto anything that was happening. A woman wearing jeans and a denim vest over a black Rolling Stones T-shirt opened the door and ushered me inside. I remembered Jameson handing me a glass of water and asking her to take care of me.

"What's your name, honey?" she asked, as if talking to a child while also encouraging me to drink the water.

"C-Carina," I said, my voice sounding hollow to my own ears.

"Well, everything's gonna be fine. You hear me, Carina? You're okay. Just you settle down. The boys'll see you right."

I nodded and took deep breaths, trying to still the nausea building in my stomach.

"Can I get you some food? Are you warm enough?" the woman asked.

I took another sip of the water and tried to smile, embarrassed by the fuss and the scene I was causing. "I need to use the bathroom, if that's okay?" I said.

"Of course. Go through the door and up the stairs. It's the second door on the left. Do you need me to help?"

I thanked her for the offer, but declined. I cast a quick glance at Jameson, who paced at the far end of the room while talking to someone on the phone. His tone was angry, but his words not quite registering past the pulse pounding in my ears. I gripped the banister and found the room in question. It was a bedroom, but beyond there was an attached bathroom.

I took another deep breath as I closed the door and wondered what the hell was wrong with me. My legs trembled, and I feared they would give out beneath me, so I sat on the closed lid of the toilet and rested my head in my hands.

I'd never been as scared as when the man pointed the gun at Jameson's head and told him they wanted me. A sob broke from my lips, and my breathing came in gasps. I'd always believed I was strong, that I could face anything, but I was wrong. Right now, I was so scared, but more than that, I was weak. I was powerless to do anything. I couldn't see a way out of the mess I was in. All I could think was that if I didn't go with the men, if I didn't marry Xander Caruso, then he would kill my brother, he would kill Rahat, and he would kill Jameson. I couldn't let that happen. I'd rather kill myself.

Hot tears burned my cheeks, and any semblance of self-control completely fled me. I rested my head in my hands and cried in a way I hadn't done since my father died.

A knock sounded on the bathroom door. I sat bolt upright, ashamed to be found in the state I was in. A part of me hoped it was Jameson and that he would promise to make everything okay, to keep me safe, but another was mortified to think of him seeing me like this. He'd said I was nothing more than a little girl playing games, and he was right. I just hadn't known it.

"Carina," a soft voice called. "It's Kitty," she said, revealing her name to me for the first time, at least as far as I could remember.

"I'm fine," I said, even though she hadn't asked.

"Ah, sweetie, I don't think you are. I'm coming in."

The door handle turned, and Kitty entered, her face a mask of concern. She moved close and crouched down to my level on the floor in front of me. "I heard a little of what Jameson was saying on the phone," she said and gripped my hand tight in hers. "He's a good man. He'll take care of you."

I scoffed. I wanted to believe that he was, but how good could he really be? "Is he?" I asked. "How good can either of us truly be with the families we come from? The Rizzos may be on good terms with the Swash family, but that doesn't mean we're friends. If push comes to shove, Jameson will have to follow whatever the head of his family orders, and if that means I'm shipped off to live a life of torture with Xander Caruso, then that's what will happen."

Kitty looked a little taken aback by my words, but she squeezed my hand tighter in her grasp and patted the top of it with her other hand. "I ain't gonna pretend to know half of what you said, and I sure as hell don't know no Rizzo nor no Swash family, but I know my boys at Forever Midnight. Those boys will keep you safe, honey. It's what they do. And Jameson's a brother through and through. Forever Midnight's in his veins. Like I said, he's a good man. He'll take care of you."

I wanted to believe what she said, but the Jameson I knew was a Swash. He was mafia, like me. My brow furrowed, and I wondered more about Jameson and how he'd ended up living in Colorado with a biker gang. From his interaction with the brothers, as he called them, they were obviously close. I'd already observed them to be his true friends, but how had that happened? Why was he here, and why hadn't I seen him in all the years since my father's funeral? I'd seen his brother countless times. The questions swirled in my mind. I wanted to ask Kitty, but knew she didn't have any answers. Instead, I wiped the tears from my eyes and huffed out a deep breath. I was about to stand when Jameson appeared in the doorway.

"Everything okay?" he asked.

An irrational anger flared when I saw his face. Every inch was flooded with concern, as if he knew how weak I was.

Kitty patted my hand and rose. "I'm gonna head to the store and leave you two to talk," she said and pushed past Jameson out into the bedroom. "Get some rest. You both look like you need it."

I cleared my throat and rose from the toilet seat. Without saying a word, I turned on the tap and rinsed my face. The bite of the water made me realize I had a small cut on my face. I winced as I blotted it with a towel.

Jameson came into the bathroom and took the towel from my hands. "Everything okay?" he asked again.

I wanted to scream and shout and push him away. But I didn't. Not really. I wanted the opposite of that, but couldn't face another rejection. Tears flooded my eyes again. "You tell me," I said, angry at the way I was acting.

He cupped my face with his hand and wiped away my tears. A shiver crept down my spine at his touch. My core ached. I wanted him, needed him to help me forget. To feel nothing but the sensation of having him inside me.

"I won't let Caruso have you," he said.

"Do you really think you can stop him?" Without thinking, I stepped forward and brushed his lips with my own. He swallowed hard and stared at me. "Please," I said. "Don't push me away. Not now."

"I won't take advantage of you when you're vulnerable."

"You won't be," I said. "I'll be taking advantage of you."

Before common sense could take over me, I reached for the hem of my top and lifted it over my head. His eyes dipped to my breasts and my flesh tingled. I kicked off my shoes and unfastened my jeans before wriggling my hips and pushing them down. I stepped out of them, kicked them away and stood in front of Jameson in nothing but my underwear: a lilac sheer satin bra and panty set.

"Take everything off," was all he said, and so help me, I obliged.

I stood stark naked before him in the bathroom while he remained fully clothed. He did nothing but look at me. I'd never felt more exposed, but my core clenched with growing need, and I was getting wetter by the second.

"A body this beautiful should never be covered," he said after a moment, and I felt my cheeks flush. He stepped forward and lifted me, spinning me around and moving me to the bedroom.

He placed me on my feet and dropped to the ground before me. I shivered and moaned as he planted a soft kiss on my stomach. His hands touched the back of my calves. He trailed them up my legs, cupped my bottom, and squeezed tight. My legs faltered, and I tried not to stagger forward towards him.

While one hand continued its journey and came to a rest on the small of my back, the other trailed a strong path all the way down the front of my body. His fingers slid over my mound. I shivered and cried out in need as he pressed them inside me. My core clenched around them, wishing them deeper, and my hands fell to brace myself on his shoulders.

Jameson made a low growling sound. He looked up at me, and his lips twitched. He removed his fingers and lifted them up to show me. Like I didn't already know how fucking wet I was.

"Lick them clean," he demanded.

Fuck, help me, I wanted to. I wanted to taste just how wet he'd made me by barely doing a damn thing. I pulled his fingers into my mouth and swirled my tongue around them.

"I need you to fuck me," I said, and shuddered under the weight of my own need.

Instead of answering, he moved his head to my breast and gently kissed my nipple, making both harden into stiff peaks. The palm of his hand cupped my breast, and he sucked hard, sending ripples of pleasure shooting down my spine. He released my nipple from his mouth with a popping sound. The bereft feeling that flooded my chest was short-lived when he grabbed my nipple again between his fingers, plucking and twisting until I cried out in pain. Bolts of pleasure rushed straight to my core, and my clit ached as much as the tight bud of my nipple.

"Fuck!" Jameson said. Suddenly, he stood, lifting me with him.

The firmness with which he pushed me down on the bed turned me on even more.

I sucked in a breath when he spread my legs, and his fingers explored the wetness between my thighs, rubbing at my opening with agonising slowness. My wetness poured out, and he pushed inside. My breath hitched as they delved deep, scissoring, and thrusting. His thumb circled my clit, and I thrust into his magical hand.

He trailed his tongue up my body and finger fucked me harder. He nipped my nipple and then sucked it into his mouth. Through heavy eyelashes, his eyes bored into mine with heat and lust. A low grumble built in his chest, and he bit my nipple. Hard.

My head fell back. I ran my hand over his short, dark hair and pushed him tighter to my breast while rocking into his fingers.

"You like that?" he asked and bit me again. My nipple tightened further, pleading for more erotic pain.

"Yes," I gasped. "B-but I want... I need you to fuck me, Jameson."

He stopped what he was doing and straightened. "Do you think you're ready for me?" he said, which caused me to lift my head and look at his crotch.

His member popped completely erect, pressed tight against his belly by the remaining bounds of his jeans. I gasped, worried that it was bigger than my arm. I didn't think I'd ever be ready. But I also thought I'd die if I didn't feel him inside me.

"Yes," I said. "Fuck me. Now."

He raised an eyebrow and lifted my legs to rest on his shoulders. There was no teasing, no testing to see if he'd fit. He pushed himself in. I cried out. The pressure built, and I felt fit to burst, but still, he pushed in deeper, and deeper... and deeper, widening me with his girth.

"Oh, fuck me!" I screamed; not sure I could take it.

"Halfway there," he said, and I realized my earlier assessment had been way off. This was him taking things easy.

My heart raced. "It won't fit," I said.

"You can take it. And when you do, I'm gonna fuck you hard." He grabbed hold of my ass, and pulled me closer, filling me even more. "Now relax and accept me."

Easy for you to fucking say!

I bit my lip. I'd never been more aware of my body, and it felt electric. I wanted to be able to take all of him. I needed him to fill me. He thrust deeper. I tossed my head back and stifled another scream.

"One more push," he said as a pang of nervousness flushed my body.

I closed my eyes and gasped, not knowing whether it was pleasure I felt or pain. He slid deeper inside.

"Oh, God!"

He pulled back, slowly, before pushing inside again. The same slow, measured movements over and over, allowing my body to accept him.

"Fuck! That's an incredible fucking pussy," he groaned.

His hands gripped my hips. He held me tight, stretched me, filled me. He pulled back and then slammed forward. I screamed, unable to stop myself. His cock claimed every depth of my core as he fucked me hard. Need, pleasure, and pain shook my whole body. My core clenched greedily around his cock, wanting everything it gave me. He plunged into me, again and again, taking me hard and fast. I bucked into him, willing him deeper still, fighting to take everything he offered me.

His fingers pressed into my clit. He tweaked and teased

mercilessly. My body was on fire, everything throbbed and pleaded for release. I'd never felt anything like it.

My eyes rolled in my head, my body tensed, and I exploded. Hard. My orgasm crashed over me with an intensity I'd never known. Still, he didn't stop. If anything, he fucked me harder. Just when I thought my orgasm would end, another followed in its wake. Only then did Jameson still, holding himself hard and deep within me. I lay there panting, trembling with the intensity of my climax. Jameson laid soft kisses on my chest and allowed my breaths to calm before slowly withdrawing. As he pulled out, I realized just how big he'd been.

He stepped back, fully clothed, where I was completely naked. I pushed myself up on my elbows on the mattress and licked my lips.

"I want to lick you clean," I said, and Jameson smiled.

CHAPTER NINE

Jameson

Although I'd wanted to, I hadn't planned on fucking Carina. I'd wanted to protect her, to keep her safe. When the Jeep rolled, and the Feral Son demanded I hand her over, I knew then and there, I never could. So help me fucking God. I never wanted her out of my sight again.

I... I just... I just wish I fucking knew what to do. I'd run away from my life in New York for a reason, but this whole thing with Carina was sucking me back in. It was the last thing I wanted, but I knew in that instant that I would do whatever I had to. No matter the personal cost.

The woman I carried from the bathroom was completely different from the one I'd seen inside. She'd turned from someone scared and vulnerable to someone so completely sure of her body and the power she held over me. She knew exactly what she did to my cock and enjoyed watching me squirm. I'd briefly wondered if she'd be intimidated, standing completely naked in front of me when I was fully clothed. I should have known better; she was anything but. I knelt and probed her pussy. Being exposed made her slick and wet. I trailed my hand down the full length of her body, looking for any trace of fear or doubt, any change of mind. There was none.

Desire twisted like a knife in my gut, and I just had to feel that tight pussy wrapped around my cock. She had no clue what she was asking for. I'd had women up and leave at the size of my cock, but seeing how wet she got, I knew she could take it.

I want to lick you clean, she'd said.

Fuck! She was heaven. I couldn't help the smile that spread across my face. She was also insatiable.

I clasped my hand around her neck and claimed her lips while pulling her to the edge of the bed. I stood in front of her with my cock almost level with her face. She didn't hesitate. She looked up into my eyes as though challenging me, opened her mouth, and licked at the fucking tip of my head like it was a fucking lollipop. I shuddered and moaned. She did it again.

Her eyes fluttered closed as though she was the one being pleasured. She took her time, licking every fucking inch of my rigid flesh. I wanted to pound into her mouth, and find release, but

I wanted to watch her suck me even more.

She wrapped her hand around my cock and pumped slowly before finally drawing me into her mouth, slurping at my shaft with eager wet lips. My thighs trembled, and I growled in appreciation. She groaned and shifted on the bed a little, and I knew she was getting wet all over again. I stared at her perfect breasts and tight pink nipples. I wanted to squirt all over them. She was so fucking perfect, so round, so soft.

"Fuck! That feels… just… just like that."

Carina moaned and with agonizing slowness, she took me further into her mouth. She used her hands, her mouth, her tongue. She fondled my balls. Her every focus was on pleasuring me, and fuck was she! I felt as hard as a rock and fit to explode. She opened her mouth further. This time, I couldn't help but push inside, but I kept my movement gentle. She could work her way up to taking me fully. Even though I almost fucking came when she hummed against my cock.

She must have noticed as she hummed some more and sucked me in as deep as she could. I couldn't hold back any longer and tried to pull away, but she pulled me back, sucking on my rod with animalistic fervor.

"Oh fuck," I said and shuddered, spilling everything I had into her perfect mouth.

She lapped up my cum greedily, and when she pulled back and wiped the bottom of her lip suggestively with her finger, I knew she wasn't done with me yet. My cock knew too and instantly started to harden. I lifted her head and studied her face, flushed and needy.

~

Insatiable didn't even come close to describing Carina. We spent countless hours holed up in the bedroom. I'd never felt pleasure like it. Given the option, I would never leave the room. I lay on my back, resting while Carina tucked herself into my side. After a while, she shifted, turning on her side to face me. I looked down at her perfect face. Her cheeks were still flushed, and her pupils were wide. She had a satisfied tilt to her smile.

"Why are you here? In Colorado, I mean," she asked, her wide eyes brimming with questions. "Who are you? Why have I never seen you in London when your brother comes all the time?"

I stiffened at her words. I'd become accustomed to never speaking of my past.

She must have sensed my discomfort as the sheet rustled as she sat up in bed and swept her long brown hair behind her ear. "I'm sorry," she said. "I shouldn't pry."

I growled and huffed out a deep breath. When I'd left New York all those years ago, I thought that if I never talked about who

I was or where I came from, then my past would stay exactly that... my past. But if there was one thing I'd learned over the years with Forever Midnight, it was that you can't keep things buried forever. Thea had fled from her abusive family, and they'd caught up with her. Amber had fled from Caleb after her attack, unsure if he or her attacker was the father of her baby, and Hope had hidden out for a decade in witness protection after witnessing a murder, leaving a broken Bono behind. They'd all run away from their problems, but one way or another, they'd all been forced to go back and face their past, and look how happy and free it had made them.

I chuckled and shook my head at the realization that I was the girl in this situation. Not that there was anything wrong with that, but it made me realize that Carina wasn't the little girl playing games. I was. The last seven years had been a big fucking game of hide and seek. I wasn't ready to embrace my past life, but maybe now would be a good time to accept that it happened.

"You have nothing to apologize for." I took a deep breath. "I'm Jameson Swash," I said, "and I'm the rightful head of the Swash family." I chuckled at my admission. I almost felt like I was putting my hand on my heart and confessing to being an alcoholic at some AA meeting. "For generations, my family served as second in command to the Bianchis."

Carina tilted her head curiously. "I thought you said that Manuel Caruso was second in command."

"He is. He was appointed following my father's death. I was set to take over on my thirtieth birthday."

Carina swallowed back a gulp and pulled the sheet tighter around her. "What happened?" she asked.

"I left. Turned my back on the life and handed control of everything to Jordan."

A knock sounded on the door, making us both jump. Carina quickly dashed from the bed, grabbed her clothes, and rushed into the bathroom. I stifled a smile while calling out, asking who it was.

"Put your fucking twiglet and berries away," Lucky called from outside, making me chuckle. He always did have a way with words. "Caleb and Cane will be here in a few minutes."

CHAPTER TEN

Jameson

"What have you learnt?" I asked as soon as we entered Kitty's living room.

Cane was sitting in an armchair, and Caleb was perched on the windowsill. They both nodded their heads in greeting to Carina, but Cane gave me a strange look when he realized I was holding her hand.

"The Feral Sons were hired to retrieve Carina," Caleb said, stating the obvious. "The guys we talked to weren't sure who hired them, but they were 100% fucking sure it was some bigwig in New York."

I nodded.

Carina released my hand and flopped down on the sofa. "Could he really have traced Rahat's phone and found me?" she asked, the tone of her voice making it clear that she'd never really believed that such a thing was possible.

Cane shrugged. "Given our past interactions with your contact in New York, it's possible they put eyes out everywhere and just got fucking lucky," he said.

I ran my hand over the top of my head and asked Cane if I could use his phone. What we really needed was to know what was going on in the background. I had no idea what Jordan, Gabriel, or Xander were currently up to. We'd need to move Carina out of Castle Rock and somewhere safe soon. The problem was, without knowing what was going on, there was no way of knowing where safe was. Without wanting to hide anything from my brothers, I put the phone on speaker and waited for Jordan to pick up.

"Manuel's dead and Xander's setting up a meeting to gain the final support he needs before staking his claim for his father's role," Jordan said without a word of greeting.

Fuck! That wasn't good. "Where is he now?"

"New York."

Normal children would want to be with their father during his final days. They wouldn't be traveling the globe in an attempt to take over his job. But that's typical of the way mafia families work, especially one like the Carusos. "Will he get it?" I asked.

Jordan huffed down the line. "Gabriel has already been on the phone," he said instead of answering my question. "He doesn't see how he can withhold Carina from Xander any longer. He wants her to call him so they can talk through her options."

I rubbed my head and glanced at Carina as she sat on the couch, listening, and staring at me with a wide-eyed, worried look on her face. "Are there any?"

"If Xander takes over as second in command, no."

I flopped my head in my hand and rubbed at my tired eyes. "I won't let him take Carina," I said.

"Then you'll have every soldier under every caporegime after you. You're talking about thousands of men. It won't be like last time when Dolmilo was on his own," he said, referring to the mob killer who'd come after Bono's fiancée after she put him behind bars for ten years. "You do have one option," Jordan said, and I knew exactly what he meant.

"That's not an option." I closed my eyes and huffed out a deep breath.

Pressure built, and I felt the entire weight of my family responsibilities fall on my shoulders. Manuel Caruso had taken on the role of second in command when our father had died. At twenty-two, I'd been too young to be considered a candidate for underboss, leaving the position free for Manuel to assume. But both our families knew. The second I turned thirty, I'd have had a claim to the mantle and could have challenged him for it. Instead, a year before that happened, I'd turned my back on my life, and I'd never looked back, never even thought about it. Until now.

"Jameson," Jordan said along the line.

"We'll see what Gabriel has to say to Carina before making any decisions," I said and hung up.

Carina stood from the sofa and crossed the room to stand beside me. "You can't get me out of this. No one can," she said, more of a statement of fact than a question.

"What does any of this mean?" Caleb asked.

"Don Bianchi is the current mafia boss in charge of at least twenty-eight families across the globe. Manuel Caruso was his second in command. Now that he's dead, Xander is positioning himself to take his place. If he succeeds, there's nothing any of us can do to keep Carina from him."

"Fucking bullshit," Cane said.

Carina closed her eyes, sat back down on the couch, and shook her head. "Why did Gabriel even try to send me away? What was the point when he knew it was fruitless?"

I thought about her words for a moment before everything became clear. Gabriel and Jordan knew exactly what they were doing in sending Carina to me. I paced the room, my fists clenched.

Rage built like an inferno inside me. My heartbeat thumped in my ears. Unable to stop myself, I walked over to the door and punched it. My hand throbbed, but I punched it again, satisfied this time when the wood cracked.

Caleb stood and placed a calming hand on my shoulder. "We'll figure things out, even if we have to send the two of you to fucking Alaska for a few years."

Fuck!

I should never have made any form of bargain with my brother. If I'd learned anything over the years, it was that family couldn't be trusted. I guessed my brothers at Forever Midnight had made me start to forget that one simple fact. I was the elder brother. Jordan deferred to me. But I hadn't wanted to wield that power, and instead I'd agreed to owe him one for all the help he gave in protecting Hope. I should have bypassed him and gone to the other families myself, but that would have put me exactly where I am now. The worst thing was, I'd fucking fallen for it. Hook, line, and sinker.

Fuck!

Carina stood, came over to me, and reached out to take my hand. "It doesn't matter. I'll do what I have to do to keep peace among the families. It's not up to you to keep me safe when I can just go to Xander and keep everyone safe. You, Rahat, Gabriel. I don't want this to go on any longer. I don't want to see anyone hurt."

She flashed me a weary smile before straightening her back and lifting her chin. I fucking loved that about her. She didn't realize how strong she truly was. I was easily twice her size with steam practically coming out of my nostrils; if she married Xander, she faced a horrendous future, but she stood and faced me without a shred of fear on her face.

"You honestly have no idea who I am," I said and glanced from Cane to Caleb, knowing that they didn't either.

Carina's eyes bore into my soul as if she could see the truth inside. Maybe she could. Goddamn it. Carina made me feel... I don't know what the fuck she made me feel besides confused. I let out a deep breath and tried to make sense of my thoughts and find peace with the decision I'd already made.

"I came to Colorado to escape exactly the life you lead," I said after a moment. "The manipulation and games. I came because it's a good place to find out what you're made of." Anger bubbled to the surface again. I'd found the perfect woman: strong, sexy, with intelligent, thoughtful eyes, but the only way to be with her was to claim my old life back. The life I'd vowed to leave behind forever. "I'm Jameson Swash," I said, echoing my earlier words to her in the bedroom. "I'm the rightful head of the Swash family. If I go back and claim my rightful place, I can forbid Xander Caruso from even looking at you."

CHAPTER ELEVEN

Carina

I couldn't make sense of what I was hearing, and I wished I'd taken more of an interest in the family business over the years. But the year after Mum had died, Dad had been inconsolable. He'd ranted about how the family business had led to her death. How he'd hated the life and wished he'd never been born into it. It took both of them from me, so I'd tried to stay as uninvolved as possible. If what Jameson was saying was true, then apart from the Don's family, no other held more power than his. And he'd walked away from it all... decided to live like some biker dude in Colorado. I could understand that, but what I couldn't understand was how he'd be willing to go back to save me.

My thoughts churned over everything that had happened, and my chest tightened. Gabriel and Jordan had done this deliberately. Jameson wanted to be free, and I'd been sent as some sort of honey trap to lure him back. He should hate me, not want to save me.

"I won't let you do it," I said, surprising myself. "You have a life here. You were right to want to be away from all this crap. I'm not going to let you go back. Not for me." Jameson opened his mouth to protest, but I raised my hand to stop him. "As the wife of the underboss, everyone will treat me with respect."

"Except Xander Caruso," Jameson said, making me wish that the world would just open up and swallow me into a black hole.

Before I had the chance to respond, the door opened and everyone jumped to their feet, only to relax when Rex walked in with Rahat as well as Kitty and Lucky, the biker I'd briefly met when we were run off the road.

Rahat rushed straight across the room and pulled me in for a hug. "You okay?" she asked. I wanted to break down in tears and tell her I wasn't. Instead, I hugged her tight. She stroked my hair and held me close for a while.

"I'm going to New York to marry Xander Caruso," I said as soon as I pulled back.

"The hell you are!" Jameson growled.

"I'm with the big man," Rahat said. "You are *so* not marrying that psycho."

"It's my choice to make," I said, resisting the urge to start crying.

Rahat pulled me in for another hug. "Let's not go to New York. I have some money saved. We could head to Vegas, or better yet, the Outer Hebrides. No one will ever find us there."

I couldn't help but smile at the thought of Rahat on a small Scottish Island. "And what would you do there?" I asked. "The population is probably less than thirty thousand. That's nowhere near enough eyes fawning over you."

She smiled. "Maybe not, but you can be damn sure every set would be. Besides, I heard they have the best internet connection in the whole of the UK. I'll be just fine."

I huffed out a deep breath and shook my head. "It's a nice idea," I said. "But no, for everyone's sake, I have to marry Xander." As I said the words, I knew just how true they were. Xander's father hounded our family until my mother drank herself into an early grave. I could understand the pressure she felt now. I couldn't do that. I couldn't see Gabriel hurt or punished for my rebellion, but most of all, I couldn't force Jameson back into a life he hated.

"Enough!" Caleb stood from his perch on the windowsill and commanded the attention of the room. He'd been so quiet while we'd talked, I'd almost forgotten he was here. "Don fucking Bianchi may be some fucking big time boss in New York, London, and who the fuck knows where else, but he isn't in charge here.

I fucking am, and if push comes to shove, I'll walk right up to Xander Caruso and put a fucking bullet in his head before I see either of you do something you don't want to. Now everyone, sit the fuck down, and we'll run this through from the beginning. I want to know everything, the names of the families, the power they hold, and most of all, how the fuck this all started. Maybe if we start to fucking talk things through, we'll find a solution without the need of any fucker playing some sort of sacrificial hero."

Cane burst out laughing, and Lucky followed suit. "You'd make one hell of a fucking motivational speaker," he said after he'd settled.

"Yeah," Lucky echoed. "We should get him on the fucking circuit. He'd make a killing."

"I'll fucking kill *you* fuckers if you don't knock it off," Caleb said.

Everyone calmed down after that. Caleb moved the conversation to the dining room, where Kitty brought everyone beers and snacks. For the first time in my life, I sat at a table and discussed my future as if I had some say in my own destiny. It was strangely refreshing to be asked my opinion on things and not to be ordered around. It also hardened my resolve. Jameson had a good life in Colorado with good friends who loved him. No matter what, I'd never let him give that up.

CHAPTER TWELVE

Carina

The night wore on, but nothing was resolved. We just went around and around in circles. It was clear to everyone that we only had two options. Either Jameson returned to the life he hated, or I returned and married Xander Caruso. It was better to accept my fate and get on with it than sit around wallowing, wishing Jameson and his friends could come up with some last-minute miracle. Even though I wished with all my heart that they could come in at the last minute and swoop in to save me.

After a while, I excused myself from the room, feigning tiredness and the need to refresh and have a shower. But as soon as I was alone, I grabbed the phone from its cradle, took it upstairs with me, and called Gabriel, asking him to arrange for me to get to New York.

I sat on the bed, wondering how I'd escape the house

unnoticed when a soft knock sounded at the door. Rahat entered. Before she'd had the chance to step two feet into the room, I broke down in tears.

"It's all going to be okay," she said, pulling me in for a deep hug.

My tears flowed freely. I tried to compose myself and wiped them from my eyes, but they kept returning. I knew what I had to do.

"It's all going to be okay," she said again.

Rahat had been my friend for almost 15 years, since we both started secondary school at eleven. We sat next to each other on the very first day in form room. I'll never forget how she flicked her hair behind her ear, introduced herself, and then barraged me with information about the game Final Fantasy VII and how funny Don Corneo's Mansion was. I had no idea what she was talking about at the time, but we spent every weekend together over the next few months helping me find out. Those were some of the best days of my life. I briefly wondered if I'd ever see her again. I held on tighter and allowed the tears to fall freely again as I decided the best way to keep her safe was to let her go.

I took in a deep breath and pulled back, steeling my resolve. I smiled and laughed away my silliness. "I'm just being dramatic. Everything will be fine. They'll find a way." I ran my hands over the top of my head and through my hair while looking at the bed. "I think I'm just tired. I need some rest. I... I just don't think I'm in any state to deal with anything at the moment. I should get some sleep."

Rahat patted my hand before standing. "You need me to get you a drink or anything."

I shook my head, and she turned to leave. "There is one thing," I said, making her hand stall on the doorknob. "I don't think I can face anyone for a while, especially Jameson. Can you just keep everyone away?"

Rahat flashed me a warm smile. "I'll do my best," she said before leaving, closing the door tight behind her.

I waited a few minutes, listening to be sure she'd gone downstairs before moving and setting the scene. I wiped away the remains of my tears and searched through a few of the cupboards in the room. Finding the extra blankets and pillows I'd hoped were stashed somewhere, I positioned them beneath the covers on the bed to make it look like I was sleeping. After shifting them around for a few minutes, satisfied they looked sufficiently like a human form, I gave a sharp nod of my head and moved towards the window.

My heart pounded as I looked outside into the dreary night. It had been a long time since I'd climbed out of a window. I just hoped I still had the agility to pull it off. As soon as I opened the window, I was hit by an earthy blast mixed with ozone. Clouds gathered overhead with the promise of rain to come. Hopefully, I'd be under shelter before the storm hit.

As I'd hoped, the porch I'd noted when in the room earlier extended beyond my window and all the way around the house. I climbed outside, being careful not to make any noise and to pull the window shut behind me. Lights from below betrayed the location of the ground floor windows. I shifted around, edging along the porch, grateful that it held my weight, until the lights were behind me, and I could be reasonably certain I wasn't about to drop down in front of everyone. Still, I debated for a few seconds, lying flat and poking my head out to be sure, but the image of me slipping headfirst over the edge put paid to that idea. Instead, I tried to ignore the little voice inside my head telling me to go back inside, turned around, and gripped the ledge before lowering myself down. I dangled above the ground for what seemed an eternity. The drop beneath me seemed impossibly far. My heart felt fit to burst, and my arms protested every wasted second until I finally dropped, holding back a scream and instantly dropping to the ground in a crouch.

I glanced at the road, and my destination, but something stilled my step. I'd prepared myself to leave without a backwards glance. I'd wanted to sever the ties that bound me to those indoors. To go and never look back, but I pictured the concern on Rahat's face the last time I saw her. That morphed into Jameson's frustration and anger, but also that certain glint in his eye that he had when he looked at me, and only me.

Unable to resist, I choked back a sob and inched towards the nearest window. It looked into the dining room where everyone was still talking, still going round and round in circles with little to no hope of finding a way to help me.

Jameson was sitting next to Caleb. I couldn't hear the words he said, but I could see the resolve on his face. It was that resolve that made me certain I was doing the right thing. It was a look that told me he was ready to give up everything to help me. There was not a chance I could let that happen.

A lump formed in my throat, and I had to resist clearing it for fear of being discovered. I know I needed to leave, but my legs were weak, not seeming to want to work. But time was running out. I needed to be gone. I had a rendezvous to make, and every second of delay brought my escape closer to discovery.

With one final, tearful glance, I mouthed goodbye to Jameson when what I'd really wanted to mouth was 'I love you'. I turned and slipped away into the night, concealed by the shadows of an old Douglas Fir tree and the neighbouring properties.

CHAPTER THIRTEEN

Jameson

Fuck!

I wanted to punch the wall again or slam my fist through the table. I glanced at each of my brothers in turn, Cane, Caleb, Rex, and Lucky. I would do anything for each of them, but a certainty welled within me, I would do more for Carina. I'd known it from the second I saw her, and the second I placed my hand on her leg to comfort her in the car, the notion had sealed itself around my heart.

I thought back to the conversation we'd been having. Carina knew nothing of her family's past and how they connected to the Carusos. She'd known nothing about the events that plagued her mother. I couldn't help but draw parallels to their situations. Things were different then. The Russos had more power, and the consigliere had mediated, deciding that her mother was free to choose what she wanted. No such role existed within our ranks now, and even if it did, and by some miracle Carina could choose, would she be hounded for the rest of her life? Would she be driven to drink herself to death? The thought was unbearable.

Everyone was tired. Exhaustion shone on each and every face. We'd been at this for hours, and we all knew there was no way we had the power to get Carina out of marrying Xander. Well... they didn't. But I did. I knew what I had to do, but first, we all needed to follow Carina's lead and get some sleep.

My eyes drifted to Rahat, who sat next to Rex, her hands entwined with his. It brought a smile to my face. She'd been a good friend to Carina, and hopefully that friendship would continue for many years to come. And Rex, well... it was obvious from the look in his eyes that he was smitten by her.

Rahat must have sensed my gaze as she looked at me with a strange mixture of fear and concern. Maybe I had been too harsh on her before. I flashed her a weak smile, which she returned.

"I'm tired," I said, standing from my place at the table. "We all are. I think we should call it a night and get some rest," I suggested before adding that we could start again in the morning with fresh thinking heads.

Rahat jumped to her feet as soon as I made my way towards the door, stepping between me and it, and looking more than a little nervous whilst doing so. "Carina wanted to be alone, remember?"

I resisted a heavy roll of my eyes. I could understand Carina wanting to be alone, and even needing some space from me, but that was hours ago. Things change. "You go up and see if she's awake. Even if she isn't, let her know I'm coming up to sleep. We don't have to talk if she doesn't want to."

A flash of uncertainty flashed over Rahat's face, but after a moment, she nodded her agreement and left.

Caleb rose and clapped his hand on my shoulder. "We'll figure things out."

"Are you headed back home?" I asked, choosing to move on from his comment and studying his face to etch every detail in my mind. His gruff face had softened no end since he'd met Thea, and even more so since Toni had arrived. I was glad he'd found someone to love and care for, someone that gave his life purpose. They all had, apart from Rex and Lucky. Hopefully, one day they would too. Maybe Rahat could even be that person for Rex.

As the thought echoed in my mind, her panicked voice shouted from above, "Carina's gone!" She'd barely made it to the top of the stairs before I'd rushed to meet her, my brothers barely a step behind. "She's gone."

I pushed past Rahat and entered the room. The bedding had

been pulled back to reveal a mound of blankets shaped to mislead any quick glance that Carina slept in the bed. My fist clenched and I growled. She'd gone. Left. She'd done exactly what I'd planned to do: slip away and accept my fate. Well, she had another thing coming if she thought this was the end of it. There was not a chance in hell I'd leave her to marry Xander.

"I should have known." Rahat shook her head and glanced at me; her eyes wide. Something must have shone in my eyes as Rex stood protectively in front of her, pulling her close behind him. He raised his hand, about to speak, but I sighed and silenced him with a hand of my own.

"You couldn't have," I said to Rahat, trying to keep my voice soft so as not to spook her further. "She didn't want any of us to know what she was up to."

I moved over to the window and noted how the lock wasn't in place. She must have climbed outside and dropped to the ground floor below. Rahat had returned downstairs after speaking to her over three hours ago. She could be anywhere by now, but maybe there was still a chance to catch up with her and stop her from doing something even more stupid.

My restless legs wanted to run out the door and rush to... anywhere, but knew I had to think logically. In my heart, I knew she had to be on her way to New York. It would take her at least an hour to get to an airport, then another to get through check-in. If she had got on a flight in those two hours, she'd still be in the air for another three.

"What do you want us to do?" Caleb's voice asked from the doorway.

I turned to answer and noticed the telephone resting on the bedside table. It wasn't in a cradle, and I realised Carina must have snuck it upstairs with her. I picked it up and pressed redial, knowing there was only one person she could have called.

"Where's Carina?" I asked as soon as Gabriel answered.

"Who is this?"

"Jameson Swash."

I could feel the tension emanating through the pause on the line as he took in my words. Besides my brother, I hadn't had any contact with anyone from my own life in years.

"She was picked up at a private airport outside of Franktown about twenty minutes ago.

I closed my eyes and tried to still the rage that simmered at his words. "Turn the plane around," I said through gritted teeth.

"I would if I could."

A realisation struck at his words. "You didn't send the flight, did you?"

"Xander--"

"Get your fucking ass over to meet it when it lands."

"I'm in London."

I opened my eyes and glanced at my brothers, who stood, listening and waiting for me to finish and tell them what we needed to do. I rubbed at my head. Exhaustion clouded my thoughts. "Call Jordan. Give him the details of the flight and tell him I'm on my way. Then get yourself to New York."

I ended the call before he had the chance to respond, certain in the knowledge he would do as I'd asked. "Can you get us all a flight?" I asked Caleb. "Charter a plane if it's quicker."

Caleb nodded and left the room.

"I'll call Bono and get him to meet us," Cane said. This time, I didn't disagree.

"I'll be down in a minute." The words were seen as the dismissal I'd intended them to be, and everyone left me alone. I looked at the phone in my hand. I was going back in. The life I'd left had caught up to me. After all these years, I still remembered the number I needed to call. "I need to speak to Don Bianchi," I said as soon as someone answered. "Tell him it's Jameson Swash."

CHAPTER FOURTEEN

Jameson

There's a feeling in the air of New York that I've never felt anywhere else. Maybe it was the fact that I was home, or that over eight million people surrounded me, teeming with energy.

The morning sun shone an orange glow over the tall buildings in the distance. The city was said to never sleep, but at this time of the day, it truly came alive. People were going about their business with little to no knowledge of the lives around them, of the deals being made in the background, the crimes being committed. That's if they were lucky enough not to get caught up in them.

Despite the growing unease that plagued my every thought, I'd forced myself to get some sleep on the flight. I may never have joined the navy or army, but I was a soldier nonetheless, and like any soldier, the gift of sleeping where and when I could had been ingrained in me over a lifetime of battle.

Anticipation carried on the air as we paced across the car park to the waiting limo. When we got close, the door opened and Jordan stepped out, looking crisp and confident in his Armani suit. He motioned to the occupants of the SUV behind the limo to stay put, then started towards us. He was always better suited to the life than me. He looked a little older than I remembered. I guessed we both did. Lines now shone around his eyes that weren't there the last time I saw him, but if anything, over the years, his confidence had grown. He approached with a swagger born out of years of commanding and knowing that your every order would be obeyed. His role never weighed on his heart, the way it had mine. He was a leader, a killer if need be.

His gaze travelled over me, taking in my appearance and the jeans and biker jacket I wore. A small sneer played at the edge of his lips as his gaze moved away from me and towards my brothers. No doubt, he felt superior to them. Underestimating both their abilities and their characters by the way they dressed. He was wrong to. They were better men than either of us would ever be.

"Where is she?" I asked, skipping any sort of formal greeting.

His confident demeanour wavered for a second before he confirmed that her flight hadn't landed in New York as they'd anticipated. "She was taken directly to Xander's place in the

Hamptons," he said after a moment.

My blood boiled and my body tensed. I debated turning back around and getting straight back on the plane. "And Caruso?" I asked instead.

"Xander's here in New York. The meeting is scheduled as requested."

I nodded and turned back to my brothers. There was nothing they could do to help me here. I was about to ask them to head to the Hamptons and keep a watch on Carina when a motorcycle approached, stopping only a few feet away.

Bono smiled in greeting as he stepped off his bike and clasped my hand, before clasping those of his brothers. "You should have called me sooner," he said.

"You're here now." I smiled, hoping for the first time that everything was going to be okay. I had a plan. Now all we had to do was see if it worked.

I informed my brothers of how I thought they could best help me, and asked Jordan to give the details of where they needed to go. He motioned to the men in the SUV, calling them over before introducing them to the brothers and giving them instructions to escort them and keep them safe.

I couldn't help but smile at the look that crossed Caleb's face. There was no debate in my mind about who would be keeping whom safe, and it wouldn't be my brother's men.

I gave a nod of thanks and strode over to the limousine. Inside, I took a deep breath and composed myself. I'd asked Don Bianchi to call a meeting and Jordan had confirmed it was in place. Soon every mafia boss under his command would be arriving in New York, arriving to elect a new second in command. Xander thought he was a shoo-in for the role. He had no idea what was coming, and it gave me a slight glimmer of satisfaction knowing that was the case.

The door on the other side of the car opened, and Jordan climbed inside. "It's good to see you," he said, taking note of my appearance again. "You look good."

I scoffed. "Don't lie."

"No, seriously. The jacket suits you. But as much as I like it, you know you can't meet the others looking like this, right?"

"I know. I'll look the part I need to." Carina's life depended on it.

CHAPTER FIFTEEN

Jameson

Five hours later, a knock sounded on my bedroom door.

"It's almost time," Jordan said.

"I'll be out in ten," I answered before quickly moving to the bathroom to shower.

Minutes later, I donned an Armani suit, finished straightening the first tie I'd worn in more than seven years, and sent a quick mental call out to Carina, wishing for her safety and that everything went the way I hoped it would.

"You sure about this?" Jordan asked again when I stepped out into the hallway.

"Are you?" I answered.

He laughed and shook his head. We both knew there was a chance neither one of us would come out of this alive. Despite the situation, I couldn't help but smile in response. We'd been close once upon a time. Maybe we could be again. If we lived.

A limo took us to a nondescript office on the lower East Side. We went up the stairs side by side and stopped when we reached the top. Voices sounded on the other side of the door.

I steeled my nerves. More than anything, I needed to exude the power and authority I was born to. A fancy suit was all well and good, but I couldn't just look the part of a mafia boss. I had to be the part, and that was a role I hadn't taken on in a very long time. A role I'd never wanted.

Jordan gave me a quick nod of his head, displaying his approval. I pushed my shoulders back and opened the door. All heads turned to me. Most flashed confused expressions on their faces.

The room brimmed with a tense energy that was hard to describe. There was a sense of gravity to the situation. Some of these men hated each other, some were waiting for others to fuck up or die, so they could take their place and move up in the ranks. Others were lifelong friends. They all knew Xander's father was dead and that the spot for second in command was up for grabs. Though few would doubt that Xander wasn't a shoo-in for the job. At least until I entered the room. From the looks that crossed their faces, my presence had caused a mix of apprehension and curiosity. No doubt some were wondering about the alliances they'd formed in my absence, and whether it would be worth throwing their support behind me instead of Xander. Those that knew me well were sure of it. Especially if they remembered the favor I held in the Don's eyes.

"You remember Frank?" Jordan said, pulling me to the left of the room.

Frank stood to greet me from his place at the round table that dominated the center of the room. He shook my hand and clapped me on the back. "I can't tell you how good it is to see you," he said and gestured to Sid, who'd come up beside him. "I trust this means Xander is in for a challenge," he added.

Sid nodded. "I bloody hope so. I can't stand that guy." He shook my hand and that of Jordan's.

I smiled. "I take it my brother and I can count on your support."

Frank's eyes flashed to my brother as if looking for extra meaning in my words, but he nodded. "The Swash family has always had it, and I see no reason for that to change now." He laughed and clapped me on the back again. "Jeez, man. I half thought you were dead. Where the hell have you been?"

"I took a nice vacation." Before he had the chance to probe further, the door opened, and Gabriel stepped inside.

He caught Jordan's eye first before turning his attention to me. "I hope you know what the hell you're doing," he said, walking forward with his hand out, ready to shake mine.

"So do I."

The next few minutes were spent doing the rounds, shaking hands and exchanging greetings around the room. Despite the tense undercurrent, the atmosphere was almost jovial with a sense of camaraderie between the men. Though not every face was friendly, it appeared that few held Xander in terribly high esteem. At best, they were afraid of him.

It wasn't hard to tell when he arrived. The door swung open, and a shadow fell over the room. Voices silenced, and men took their seats around the table.

CHAPTER SIXTEEN

Jameson

My heart raced, and my jaw clenched. His face was every bit as punchable as I remembered it to be. Sensing my mood, Jordan placed a calming hand on my arm.

I locked eyes with Xander and for a brief second, I saw a glimpse of concern in his eyes before they swept across the room, taking in the other faces.

"What are you doing here?" he asked me with a sneer, plastering his face. "Only heads of family are welcome."

Jordan stood before me. "You know full well Jameson is the head of the Swash family."

Xander turned his sneer on my brother. "I think he relinquished that title a long time ago, along with any others. Either way, he leaves, or you leave."

This time, I stepped between Xander and my brother. "I'm not sure why you think you're here, but this meeting was called at my request, and the Don knows fully that both my brother and I will be in attendance. Now I suggest you sit and listen carefully to everything that's about to be said."

The room around me seemed to shrink under the weight of Xander's glare. If looks could kill, I'd be dead a million times over. But I wasn't about to back down, not when I needed to protect Carina. With unwavering focus, I matched his glare, unwilling to be the person to back down first. I felt like a storm cloud ready to break at the first provocation. Hell, half of me wanted to break and slam his head down into the table in the process.

"You're making a mistake," was all he said to me before pulling out the nearest chair and taking his seat.

When I didn't move for a moment, he turned to me and smiled. "I'll have a coffee while you're up and about," he said. His way of regaining face after being first to break our staring contest.

I didn't bother responding. Instead, I took a seat between Jordan and Gabriel.

Frank slammed his hand on the table. "Now that we're all ready," he said. "Sid, get everyone else, and then dial in Don Bianchi."

Within seconds, the large screen on the wall came to life.

At first, it flickered with the image of countless faces. Those of the bosses who hadn't made it to New York. These were soon sidelined, only to be replaced with the Don's image. He sat in an opulent garden filled with terracotta pots, pink flowering geraniums, and cacti. The sun beat down, highlighting his face in its warm glow. He removed his sunglasses and sat forward in his chair. He looked older than I remembered, with more lines around his eyes, but as strong as any seventy-year-old could hope to be. If anyone had ever exuded a commanding presence, it was the don.

"It's good to see you amongst us, where you belong." Bianchi's gaze fixed firmly on mine. "I am eager for you to state your claim," he added. "We all are."

"I object," Xander stood, slammed his fist on the table and glared at me. "He has no right."

"Sit down," Bianchi told him, his face larger than life on the screen.

It was plain Xander wanted to object further, but nobody disobeyed the don, and he wasn't someone who liked to repeat himself. Xander sat, but the glare he shot my way couldn't be clearer. It matched the glare that some of the other families' heads shot me. Half of them had assumed me dead, the other half wished it was so. That was their way. Always wrangling for power and position.

"Now," Bianchi continued. "We are all here to vote on a replacement for my dearly departed Manuel Caruso. My trusted friend for many years. May he rest in peace."

"May he rest in peace," everyone echoed.

"Two families have a valid claim, Caruso," Bianchi said, "and Swash."

Xander stood again, but Bianchi made him sit with a glance. "Forgive me, Don Bianchi. Jameson Swash surrendered any claim he had to the position of underboss over seven years ago. He has no claim."

Bianchi's eyes flashed to me through the screen. He sat back in his chair and opened the large wooden box on the table in front of him, pulled a cigar from it, and chewed on the end. Xander gulped. That was never a good sign.

To save the Don repeating himself, Espsotio, the man to Xander's right growled. "If Don Bianchi states that both Swash and Caruso have a claim to the position of underboss, then Swash and Caruso have a mother-fucking claim to the position of underboss. You understand? Now shut the fuck up."

Xander eyeballed him, but wasn't capable of keeping quiet. "I understand. My apologies again, Don Bianchi. I spoke out of turn." His gaze flashed to both me and Jordan sat beside me, and a triumphant glint appeared in his eyes. "As only the caporegime of a family can be present under such circumstances as these, I had been momentarily confused. As you have stated, Jameson Swash has every right to stake a claim to the position of underboss. His brother, Jordan, however, is unwelcome at these proceedings and as such is in forfeit of his life."

Murmurs of agreement echoed around the table and through the chat link, but the don only continued to chew on the end of his cigar.

I kept my face straight, but inside, I smiled. I'd spoken to Don Bianchi at length regarding Xander's suitability for the role. He was far too full of his own self-importance to stay within the bounds of his role, and I had no doubt he would eventually try to usurp the don's power. With my presence in the vote, and Xander's overriding need to have his own way, he had already shown a lack of respect.

"If I may, Don Bianchi," I said, and continued when he nodded. "You are correct, Xander. I do have every right to claim my father's position as underboss. A claim which supersedes your own." When he opened his mouth to object, I raised my hand to silence him. "However, you are also correct in stating I surrendered that claim more than seven years ago when I handed my family over to my brother."

"Then the matter is fucking settled," Xander said.

"It is not," Bianchi said, and all eyes returned to the screen. "I have spoken to Jameson at length and the time he has spent away affords him a unique perspective. I have therefore decided his talents are best suited in the role of consigliere. From now on, he will be my most trusted adviser, and any disputes you have will be mediated through Jameson."

A few shocked gasps and curses sounded around the room. Manuel had ended the position when he became underboss and undertook the role as a second duty for himself. No doubt Xander had thought to do the same. Underboss may be second in command and consigliere third, but the consigliere's loyalty was only to the don, and had his ear in all matters. From the way he stared at the desk, Xander was running through the implications of this in his mind.

"Enough," Xander said after a moment, slamming his hand down on the desk. "Fine, Jameson is fucking consigliere. We are here to vote on the position of underboss."

The don told us when to speak, when not to speak, and who to fucking kill. We certainly never spoke to him the way Xander just had. Everyone listening knew his days were numbered. They were just waiting for Xander to realize it himself. Manuel was no saint, but he knew his place. It was clear for all to see. He hadn't passed that knowledge onto his son.

Don Bianchi spat the end of his cigar out and waved the remains at Xander. "For someone who likes to tell others about procedure, you are forgetting one very important one yourself." The don motioned for me to continue.

"Thank you, Don Bianchi," I said. "As is custom, to ensure a fair process, any disputes against the Swash and Caruso family must be ruled on before the vote. Does anyone have an issue with Jordan Swash they would like to raise?"

"No fucking way," Xander screamed and stood, slamming his fists on the table. "Jordan has no fucking claim to the position."

"On the contrary, Don Bianchi has already stated that both the Swash and Caruso family have a claim. Are you fucking correcting the don again?" Espsotio asked, his voice like ice.

Xander's face reddened, and he looked fit to explode. His fists clenched against the table as he tried and failed to get a hold of his emotions.

"We've already established that Jordan is the head of the Swash family. His claim is as valid as your own. Your *issue* is dismissed. Now, does anyone have an issue with Xander Caruso they would like to raise?"

On cue, Gabriel smiled, thanked the don for his wisdom in appointing me, and gave Xander a pointed look. "Xander Caruso has demanded the hand of my sister in marriage. Given our family's history, I feel the demand is outrageous. I had hoped to strengthen the bond between the Russo and Swash family. Carina and Jameson have made a deep connection. A union between the two of them would be welcomed."

"Again, we have two valid claims," Bianchi said. "One, it is the role of the consigliere to mediate."

Xander's eyes darkened further. "He cannot rule for himself in this matter. His bias would be evident and invalidate his role."

A murmur of agreement echoed his words, lending them weight, but I merely smiled in response.

"I would never dream of it. It seems to me the solution is simple, Carina's mother was free to choose who she would marry, and Carina should be awarded the same opportunity. It is my belief she is currently in the Hamptons, perhaps you should arrange for her to be brought to New York where we can await her decision whether she wishes to marry me or Xander. Untouched and unharmed, of course."

Xander's face reddened, and he looked fit to explode. He stood; his fists clenched against the table. He tried and failed to get a hold of his emotions. "You're not going to get away with this," he snarled. "I'll make each and every one of you fucking pay."

Without another word, he left the room, rage etched into every inch of his bearing.

"You've made an enemy for life," Don Bianchi stated.

I nodded my head and met his gaze. "I never expected we would be friends. Do I have your permission to ensure Xander fulfils his obligation and doesn't lay a finger on Carina?"

The don studied me for a moment and smiled. "You are consigliere. It is your job to ensure your decisions are upheld and to punish those who disobey them."

"Then if you'll excuse me, I need to get to the Hamptons."

"Of course." The don briefly tilted his head at the other men around the table before asking Jordan, Espsotio, and Fred to accompany me.

Gabriel stood. "If it please--"

Before he had the chance to say another word, the don waved his hand in dismissal. "I had already assumed you would be in attendance to ensure your sister's safety."

With only a brief word of farewell, we left the meeting with the role of underboss still not voted on. If Xander acted the way I expected, the way I half feared, a vote would no longer be necessary. I suspected Don Bianchi felt the same way, and that Espsotio and Fred were chaperones to confirm my actions as required.

CHAPTER SEVENTEEN

Carina

I stared out of the window and at the beach, willing the tears to stop flowing. Under different circumstances, this would be a paradise. But for me, it was nothing more than a gilded cage. I wished with all my heart that things could have been different. That Jameson was here with me now, but that wasn't to be. Instead, I stood alone on gleaming marble floors, watching as the sun set over the Hamptons, casting a warm glow over the sprawling estate.

I sniffed and cleared my throat, wiping the tears from my eyes.

"Carina," I said, trying to add a note of determination to my voice. "You chose this. It was the only way."

Despite my best intentions, any hope of courage failed me. My heart pounded, and I tried to quell the rising panic that threatened to consume me.

Surrounded by elegance and wealth, I couldn't shake the feeling that I was being watched. That someone was lying in wait, ready to pounce when I least expected it. Every noise, every footstep, every breath of wind, reminded me that Xander could arrive at any second. What happened after that, I couldn't bear to think about. If only I could stop. Footsteps sounded beyond the room, growing louder, muffled voices sounded, and I knew beyond a shadow of a doubt that the time had come.

Still, when the door burst open, I couldn't help the shiver that ran down my spine. I turned, and there he stood.

Xander.

His face contorted in rage. His eyes locked onto mine, like a predator zeroing in on its prey. That same feeling I had in the club when his eyes first locked onto mine returned in full force. He was a bad man in every way, and he wanted to tear me apart.

"Carina," he growled, his voice low and dangerous as he stalked towards me.

My heart pounded, and blood roared in my ears. I fought my fight-or-flight instinct with everything I had. God! I wanted to turn and run, but I'd made my bed, and now I had to lie in it. For Gabriel, for Jameson. This was what I had to do.

"Xander," I replied, trying to inject confidence into my shaking voice.

He stopped mere inches from me. The scent of his cologne invaded my senses. I tried to tell myself that was why I felt nauseous.

He growled and a strange look crossed his face as if he was debating something, but whatever inner conflict warred inside his head. When he sneered, I knew his evil side had won. "You belong to me," he said.

I swallowed back the lump forming in my throat and stood tall. Using everything I had, I pushed down the fear rising inside me and let my anger take control instead. I may be forced to marry Xander, but I would never belong to him.

"I belong to no one," I spat back.

My defiance fuelled his rage. Before I could react, his hand shot out and a vicious backhand connected with my cheek.

A sharp pain exploded across my face. I staggered backwards as tears blurred my vision. The room spun, the luxurious chandeliers above me merged into a single blur of light as I struggled to remain on my feet. As I crumpled to the floor, the world around me erupted into chaos.

"Carina!" someone shouted, but the sound seemed distant, echoing through the fog of pain enveloping me. I cried out, almost believing the voice belonged to Jameson. But then he was there. He was really there. He came for me.

Jameson lunged. His fists pummelled into Xander's face. The sound of flesh hitting flesh resonated in the room, but my ears were ringing from the blow, and it all seemed far away.
I felt an arm roughly grab me, pulling me to my feet. I turned to look through blurry eyes.

"Get off her!" Cane roared, his deep voice booming through the mansion as he charged at one of Xander's men, tackling him to the ground with brute force, and dragging him away from me.

The room transformed into a whirlwind of violence as Jameson's friends joined the fray, each of them launching themselves at Xander and his henchmen with determination etched on their faces.

Jameson's friends. His true friends, I'd called them, and they were all here now: Rex, Cane, Caleb, Lucky, even some men I'd never seen before. I was so relieved, and confused, and happy... but I couldn't shake the thought from my head that they shouldn't be here. Nothing good could come out of this for Jameson.

"Carina, are you okay?" Cane shouted over the din. His brow furrowed with concern as he threw a powerful punch that sent another one of Xander's goons reeling.

"I...I don't know." My cheek throbbed with pain, and my vision still swam from the force of Xander's blow.

Amid the chaos, watching these men risk everything for me stirred something deep within my heart... Hope!

Their combined efforts began to overpower Xander and his men. Their skills and teamwork were evident in each well-coordinated attack. The room spun around me as the cacophony of grunts, shouts, and the sickening sounds of flesh meeting flesh filled my ears. My heart raced, and a deep sense of vulnerability washed over me. I needed to get away. Thinking of nothing else, I rushed forward with my limited vision focused only on reaching the door.

"Carina, watch out!" Rex shouted.

His warning came too late. Xander lunged towards me like a wild animal. His fist connected with my face, sending another shock of searing pain throughout my skull. I crumpled to the ground, my head hitting the unforgiving marble floor with a sickening thud.

"Get back!" Jameson commanded, landing one final, devastating punch that sent Xander sprawling onto the floor in front of me. The blood trickling from the corner of his mouth was the last thing I saw before oblivion overtook my senses.

CHAPTER EIGHTEEN

Carina

I blinked back confusion and sat bolt upright in the bed, taking in my unfamiliar surroundings. My head throbbed, and I struggled to remember what happened. Xander... Jameson.

"You're awake."

"Jameson," I said as his intense gaze locked on to my face. "You came for me."

"Why would you ever think I wouldn't?" he answered.

"H-how long was I out?"

"Seven hours. We're in New York."

"What?"

He laughed and inched over to the bed, sitting beside me and grasping my hand.

"The doctor checked you over. You're going to be fine. It's a mild concussion. He said you may have one hell of a headache, but other than that…"

"And Xander?"

"Dead."

I never thought my heart would soar at such news. In that moment, I felt nothing but happiness and relief, but then I realised what all this meant for Jameson. "You shouldn't have done this. It's not what you wanted." He'd worked so hard to get away from his life with the mafia. Now, because of me, he was right back in it. He must hate me, and if he didn't now, I couldn't comprehend a future where he wouldn't grow to.

"It's what's best for both of us."

"But head of your family, second in command… You'll never have the life you wanted."

Jameson smiled and squeezed my hand. "Then thank fuck that as of this morning, Jordan has taken on both of those roles." He must have seen the confusion etched on my face as he continued. "You're looking at the new consigliere. I'll be working to resolve disputes and conflicts. I can stay in Colorado and travel where needed. It's the best of both worlds."

"That's amazing news."

"Let's hope you still think so after I tell you we're kind of engaged to be married."

"If I've been out of it for the last seven hours, how on Earth did I manage to get engaged?"

"You were meant to choose either my hand or Xander's today, but with Xander out of the picture, you're stuck with me by default." Without saying another word, he lifted his T-shirt over his head and threw it on the floor. I itched to reach out and touch his sculpted flesh, but instead averted my eyes.

"I thought you were sick of games," I said, unable to keep the note of desire from my voice.

He moved towards me slowly, his eyes never leaving my face. He reached out and pulled the blankets from my body. His eyes dragged down my body and rested on my chest. I shivered under his gaze.

He flicked at my bra with practiced ease, undoing the clasp in one swift movement. His fingers traced over my shoulders and down my arms as he slid me free of the straps. My knickers soon followed my bra to the floor.

Goosebumps stood out on my flesh as, once again, I lay before him, completely naked.

He brushed the hair from my shoulder. My breath seized in my lungs and need pulsed straight to my core. My fingers itched to reach out and touch him, but I kept them firmly by my side.

"What do you want?" I asked.

"I was about to ask you the same thing?" He reached to the top of his jeans and unbuttoned them, setting free his thick, rigid cock. I imagined it pounding into me, filling me completely. Just the thought of what he could do to me had me gasping as my core clenched against nothing. Willing him inside, I licked my lips and instantly berated myself.

What the hell was I doing? No man had ever made me feel the way Jameson did, the way my fiancée did. Fiancée. I liked the sound of that, even if I never had the romantic proposal I'd always dreamed about.

He reached to the waist of his jeans and unthreaded his belt. I took a shuddering breath and relished knowing just how wet he was making me. The pulsing need between my legs intensified, and Jameson gripped my hand and brushed his thumb over the pulse point on my wrist. A small smile played at the edge of his lips, as though he was pleased to find my heart racing for him. Without a word, he pulled me into his body with my arms pressed behind me.

I felt small, encompassed in the warmth of his arms, but also safe. My whole body felt alive. I lifted my head to look into his eyes. He stared back and his lips lowered to mine. Capturing me, he thrust his tongue inside. My legs threatened to buckle, but he held me tight. There was nothing soft or gentle in his actions. Only possessive. His kiss claimed me as his hands worked to fasten my arms behind my back with his belt.

"Do you want me?" he asked, his breath like fire against my ear.

"Yes," I almost gasped. The memory of how good it felt for him to claim me circled forefront in my mind. I wanted that again. Needed it.

He lightly brushed his hands down my chest and stomach, creating a trail of goosebumps wherever they touched. Heat soared through my body. I could barely breathe when they trailed over my mound. I shuddered in anticipation.

He pulled me from the bed, flipped me around and guided me to the couch, where he bent me over the arm. My face pressed into the coarse material of the cushions. I wanted to use my hands to push me up, but they were wrapped tight in the belt behind my back, with Jameson holding onto them with one hand. The other ran a trail up my thigh.

CHAPTER NINETEEN

Jameson

Ever since speaking to Carina in the garden of the safe house, I'd planned exactly what I wanted to do, and had set things in motion to ensure they were done. And right now, that plan involved having Carina naked before me... again.

She'd sat in the bed, vulnerable yet strong and determined, and my cock had responded by becoming hard in an instant. Her bottom pointed in the air over the arm of the couch, giving me a perfect view of everything she had. She was so incredibly wet and begging for me to touch her. I obliged.

"How many men have you been in this position with?" I asked.

"Only you."

She gasped and bit her bottom lip as I ran ruthless circles around her clit, pinching and teasing without mercy. She liked it a little rough, and I liked giving her what she wanted. But on my terms. I softened my touch, knowing it would make her beg for more. With the gentlest of movement, I stroked her clit and teased her entrance with my fingers.

Carina squirmed and tried to push back onto them, but I lifted her bound arms and forced her deep into the couch, forbidding her to move.

"Please," she said after a moment.

Before she could utter another word, I delved my fingers inside, plunging them in and out and working her wetness around her throbbing clit.

She cried out when I withdrew them, begging for more. This time I licked up and down her folds, and sucked her clit roughly into my mouth. She tried to squirm, but I wouldn't release the pressure on her arms.

I teased her swollen bud before pushing inside with my tongue. Fuck! She tasted so sweet, like Halloween candy. Dangerous and delicious.

"After this, we should start planning the wedding," I said. "Are you okay with settling in Colorado?"

"Y-yes. It sounds perfect. Everything sounds perfect."

I heard the truth in her words. They made my heart sing. Everything did sound perfect.

Without another word, I released her arm and grabbed onto her hair, pulling her head back to make her look at me.

"You're mine." I claimed her lips with a brutal kiss and speared her with my cock. Pushing my way fully inside without waiting to see if she could take me. I already knew she could.

CHAPTER TWENTY

Carina

F uck! I couldn't hold back the scream that ripped from my throat. Jameson plunged into me again and again, fucking me hard. Each thrust went deeper and deeper, making me undone.

"Oh, fuck," I screamed, as I exploded with pleasure, almost blacking out. My core clenched around him. He pulled out and pinched my clit, delving inside with his fingers, while his other hand worked to untie my arms. Another orgasm rocked me.

"You're incredible," he said and slapped my ass cheek, hard. "Your ass is made for fucking." He ran his hand over the curve of my bottom and pumped his finger in and out of my pussy. "Has anyone ever fucked your ass?" he asked.

I closed my eyes and willed him to do it, even though I was afraid. "Never," I answered.

"I'll stop if you want me to." His hands spread my cheeks, and he twirled my wetness around the entrance.

I closed my eyes and enjoyed the sensations.

I gasped as a cold sensation hit me, and I realised it must be lube. Slowly, he pushed his finger inside. With my hands free, I dug them into the cushion on either side of my head.

"Relax," he said. "Remember, I'll stop if you want me to."

I calmed my breathing and tried to relax. "Fuck!" I screamed as his finger pushed all the way inside me while his thumb circled my clit.

He hooked his finger slowly and worked it in and out. "Touch yourself," he said and grabbed my hand, pushing it beneath me and between my legs. I circled my sensitive nub and probed between my folds. All the while Jameson worked his finger inside my ass.

My eyes rolled in my head, and my breaths came in desperate pants. Still, I worked my pussy while Jameson finger fucked my ass. Soon we were working in unison, pumping inside me in time with each other.

"I-I can't," I said. "D-don't stop. I'm going to come." Just as I said the words, Jameson pushed in a second finger. My senses flipped into overdrive, and my whole body flared and pulsed with delight. I screamed as my orgasm struck, sending me over a chasm as shudders racked my whole body.

Jameson withdrew and grabbed onto my hips. He let out a deep groan and pushed his cock inside my pussy, pounding me through my release. "Do you think you can take more?" he asked, and my fingers dug deep into the couch.

A strangled noise escaped my lips. I didn't know if I could, but I did know, I never wanted him to stop.

He slowed but continued moving inside me as his hands worked a trail up my back. He rubbed the back of my neck before working them back down. I moaned as he moved his finger over my back entrance. He pushed his finger inside again while his cock filled my pussy. A second finger joined the first, but this time his movements were different. I felt like a powder keg set to explode, but sensed that Jameson was keeping me on the cusp of pleasure and making sure I was relaxed and loose enough to take what he wanted to give me.

My thoughts and emotions were all a muddle. Everything inside me wanted to stay here forever… rejoicing in the knowledge that he was my forever. I wanted… no, needed to have Jameson claim every part of me. I focused on every sensation I felt, and etched them into my memory.

After a moment, Jameson removed himself from me completely. I felt the tip of his cock touch my ass. He spread my cheeks wider and pushed inside. The pressure was blinding.

I jerked away, but he clasped onto my hips and drew me closer to him. "Don't stop. Please," I screamed, though I felt fit to burst. "Don't stop."

Jameson pulled me up, so my body was flush against him, and pressed all the way inside me. He moved in and out slowly at first, but faster as my body became accustomed to this delightful yet strange intrusion. He kissed and nipped at my neck. His one hand reached around and pinched my nipples, driving me delirious with pleasurable pain. The other pinched at my swollen clit. His fingers pressed inside my pussy and circled my bud.

"I'm gonna fucking come inside your ass," he said as he pushed me closer and closer towards oblivion.

Lost in sensation, my head dropped back to rest on his shoulder. My eyes closed tight.

The orgasm that struck was unlike any other I'd ever experienced. Like a raging storm, it ripped through my being, unstoppable and relentless. Wave after wave crashed through me and a scream ripped from my throat. Every nerve ending in my body burned. I needed Jameson to stop, to set me free, but I couldn't stand the idea of him leaving me. I was paralyzed as pleasure tore through my body with Jameson's relentless actions.

He kissed me madly and muttered my name as he jerked, and

his hot seed filled me.

EPILOGUE

Carina

My heart pounded with excitement as I admired my reflection in the full-length mirror before me. If anyone had told me a month ago that I'd be settling down in Colorado and marrying a biker, I'd have laughed in their face. The stunning wedding dress Rahat had helped me pick out clung to my every curve, accentuating my figure in all the right places. The white fabric seemed magical, the way it cascaded to the ground like a waterfall of silk.

"Today's the day," I whispered, noting the silly smile that played at my lips in the mirror. "I'm marrying Jameson."

The door creaked open. Rahat glided in, looking every inch a supermodel in the blue crisscross, backless gown she had chosen as her maid of honour dress. The silky fabric was split all the way up one side, showing her off her leg to perfection. Her eyes met mine in the mirror, full of her usual sparkle of mischief and brimming with affection.

"You look amazing," she said.

I beamed. "We both do."

"Why thank you," she said and playfully spun around. Laughing.

I couldn't help but join in at the sound, but after a moment, I sobered. I'd been meaning to ask her something for a while now, but never found the right time. I'm not sure there ever would be a right time, but I needed to know.

"Rahat," I began, my tone turning serious as I turned to face her. "Are you... are you going back to London anytime soon?"

She put her hand on her hip and gave me a mock glare. "Girl!!! Are you trying to get rid of me?"

"Never," I said and smiled again. "You're like a sister to me. This past month. Always. So much could have gone wrong, and I'm sorry I never mentioned my family's ties to the mafia. I just..."

She reached out and clasped her hand in mine. "You have nothing to be sorry for," she said. "You know me. I love it when things are a little exciting."

"Exciting! I'm not sure that's the exact word I'd use."

"I would. I did." She sighed and straightened her dress. "I think

I'll be sticking around for a while yet. Rex is..."

"Exciting?" I suggested, making us both laugh.

Before I had a chance to say anything more, the door opened, and Gabriel popped his head inside. "They're ready for you," he said.

Rahat's hands enveloped mine as we walked towards my brother, who reached his elbow out for me to clasp onto. A gentle melody sounded from outside. The familiar strains of Pachelbel's Canon made my stomach flutter. This was it. It was time.

My pulse quickened at the thought of walking down the aisle towards Jameson. I took one last look across the room into the mirror. I couldn't remember a time I was this happy.

"Remember to breathe," Rahat said. "You know, slow and steady, in and out." She demonstrated, and I followed suit, inhaling deeply and exhaling slowly.

"Okay," I said, steeling myself with a final, steadying breath. "I'm ready."

"Then let's do this," Gabriel said.

We walked together, stepping out into the warm afternoon sun, our arms linked, and Rahat following only a step behind. The whispers of silk rustling against the grass filled my ears, accompanied by the soft sighs of admiration and delight.

The guests stirred from their seats. Their gazes turned towards us, drawn by the sight of the bride, her brother, and her best, most loyal friend.

"Look at them," I heard someone murmur, a note of awe lacing their voice. "Carina looks absolutely stunning."

"Jameson's a lucky man," another added.

Their words fanned the flames of my already heightened emotions. I locked ahead where Jameson stood tall and proud, his hands clasped in front of him as if he were guarding something precious.

His eyes locked onto mine. They were filled with so much intensity, so much love, they made my heart tremble.

Every step closer to him felt like a step closer to the fulfilment of every dream I'd ever held in my heart.

"Carina," Jameson breathed as I reached his side, the tender warmth of his touch steadying me like an anchor amidst a turbulent sea.

"Jameson," I whispered back.

This was the first moment of the rest of my life, one I was finally living, and I couldn't be happier.

~

Printed in Great Britain
by Amazon